The Moon Children

Beverley Brenna

Red Deer
PRESS

Published by Red Deer Press
A Fitzhenry & Whiteside Company
www.reddeerpress.com • www.fitzhenry.ca

CREDITS
Edited for the Press by Peter Carver
Copyedited by Kirstin Morrell
Cover design by Naoko Masuda
Text design by Jacquie Morris
Printed and bound in Canada by Friesens for Red Deer Press

ACKNOWLEDGEMENTS
"Blue Suede Shoes"
Words and Music by Carl Lee Perkins
© 1955, 1956 Hi-Lo Music, Inc.
© Renewed 1983, 1984 Carl Perkins Music, Inc.
(Administered by Wren Music Co., A Division of MPL Music Publishing, Inc.)
All Rights Reserved

Red Deer Press acknowledges the support of the Canada Council for the Arts, which last year invested $20.1 million in writing and publishing throughout Canada. Financial support also provided by Government of Canada through the Book Publishing Industry Development Program (BPIDP).

Canada Council   Conseil des Arts
for the Arts   du Canada

Canadä

Library and Archives Canada Cataloguing in Publication

Brenna, Beverley A.
The moon children / Beverley Brenna.

ISBN 978-0-88995-378-9

1. Fetal alcohol syndrome—Juvenile fiction. I. Title.

PS8553.R382M66 2007   jC813'.54   C2007-901183-7

Red Deer PRESS

Dedication

For Andrew and Nicholas:
May your dreams come true.

Author's Note

Natasha and Billy are imaginary characters who have disabilities similar to those of real children.

In 1990–91, 700 children from Romanian orphanages were adopted to Canada following the fall of the communist dictatorship in Romania. Many of these children had not been well cared for and suffered from malnourishment and other conditions. Through the love and care of their adoptive families, the lucky ones, like Natasha, slowly recovered from many of their challenges.

Fetal Alcohol Spectrum Disorder (FASD), a term a doctor might use to describe Billy's condition, is a disability caused by a mother's drinking alcohol during pregnancy. It is generally thought that about one in a hundred children in North America are born with an FASD, and have a variety of physical and mental challenges depending on when and how much alcohol was consumed during their prenatal life. Although fetal alcohol conditions do cause permanent brain damage, it is important to remember that children born with this condition can have lots of potential. Although he has challenges, Billy is creative, artistic, and helpful to others. Thank you to Bethany Hase and Kayla Penteliuk for their inspiring Moon Journals; thanks also to their teacher, Cathy Charlebois, for sharing her lessons in Moon Science.

The story Billy tells about how the moon got into the sky is adapted from the classic northwest coast myth and retold in Anne Cameron's picture book *How Raven Freed the Moon*. The song Billy sings, *Blue Suede Shoes* is by Carl Perkins and is well known as a song made famous by Elvis Presley.

Other thanks: to Dr. Christtine Fondse, for your work in sharing children's literature that touches the mind as well as the heart; to Dr. Linda Wason-Ellam, for your inspirational storytelling; to Beverly Palibroda, Communications and Research Co-ordinator for the Saskatchewan Fetal Alcohol Support Network, for your encouragement; to my niece Christine, for assisting with an earlier draft of the novel; to Brenda Baker and Leona Theis, for your field of energy; to the Saskatchewan Arts Board, for its financial help; to the Starfish Team, for your ongoing celebration of diversity; to Val Burke-Harland, for your endless creative drive; to my editor, Peter Carver, who believes in going for gold; to my sons, Wilson, Eric, and Connor, my mom Myra Stilborn, my mother-in-law Elma Brenna, and my husband Dwayne, for your love and support.

Chapter One

The morning after his father left, Billy went and stood on the front steps of their apartment building, as if it were any other Friday in July. The sun already felt hot on Billy's face, and he wandered into the shade. He dug with one bare toe around a dandelion growing in the dry soil against the cement foundation. Lifting his head, he caught sight of a meadowlark perched on top of the chipped, white picket fence that separated their dry grass from the house next door. It warbled its song, notes running up and down the scale, and Billy picked up a pebble and threw it half-heartedly in the bird's direction.

Dumb bird, thought Billy. What's it so happy about? The girl from one of the big houses across the street, a schoolmate whose name he couldn't remember, was sitting on her front steps, staring at the sky. He could see her past the caragana hedge that bordered her yard like a thick fence. She'd been in the other grade five class with the lady teacher. Billy had seen her sometimes at recess. He wondered what she was looking at. He turned and craned his neck, but all he saw was the ragged roof of their three-story apartment building and beyond that, between clouds, a back pocket of blue sky.

Not enough blue to make a Dutchman a pair of pants, Mrs. Schmidt would say. Billy looked carefully at the yo-yo he'd gotten for his birthday, noticing a few new chips on its shiny blue surface, and then wound it. He tried a few tricks, stealing glances at the girl to see if she might be watching him, but she wasn't. Anyway, the Typhoon wasn't working as well as it usually did. *Walk the dog. Sleeper. Shoot the Moon.* He picked out a knot in the string and tried a few more tricks, humming "Blue Suede Shoes," one of his dad's favorite tunes.

It was better once he got into the rhythm of the song, and he worked away for a few minutes without a hitch. When he stopped and looked over at the girl, she still wasn't watching him; instead, she was writing something on some paper.

He walked across the street to get a closer look. A notebook. She was writing in a school notebook. What was she doing with a school notebook when everyone knew school had been over for two weeks?

"Hey, you," he said, going up the long sidewalk towards her house. "Whatcha doing?" He noticed how, inside the hedge, the grass was green and thick, unlike his own brittle lawn. The girl looked up. He'd never noticed before how dark her eyes were. Now they seemed to shine as if they had tears in them, ready to overflow.

"How come you look like that?" he said. "Your eyes are all watery. What's wrong?"

The girl shook her head and looked back down at her notebook. He walked close enough to smell the big cabbage roses that grew in the flowerbeds on either side of the steps, and saw that she had scrawled the date, the way they did in their journals at school, and had written some sentences underneath which he couldn't read. Then she had used a pastel crayon to draw a moon just over what was clearly his red brick apartment building. He turned to look up at the sky and sure enough, there, almost beside his window on the third floor, was the moon, edging out from behind the clouds.

"Well, whad'ya know," he said. "It's the moon. An early riser."

A silly nursery rhyme popped into his head: "Hey diddle diddle, the cat and the fiddle." He bit his tongue so he wouldn't say it aloud, but he blurted it out anyway, his voice, high and sweet, quickly finding a tune.

> *Hey diddle diddle,*
> *the cat and the fiddle,*
> *the cow jumped over the moon.*
> *The little dog laughed to see such sport*
> *and the dish ran away with the spoon.*

The girl closed her notebook and put it on the top step. Billy saw that it had a yellow cover. Then she smiled—at least, he thought that's what it was, a small shadow of a smile that caught one corner of her mouth and sent it for a fleeting second into her cheek. As she bent over to put her crayons back into their case, a strand of dark hair, as feathery as a bird's wing, fell from her ponytail and across her face.

When she had collected all the crayons, she stood and opened her front door. But before she stepped inside, Billy said, "Wait. You forgot your book." He picked up the notebook and flipped through it. He saw dates, some sentences, and more pictures of the moon. The moons looked like they were in some sort of pattern, beginning with a thin crescent and growing from page to page into the pale quarter moon she'd drawn today.

"Hey, you've got all kinds of moons in here!" he exclaimed.

There was that half-smile again. Then she snatched her book and disappeared inside the big white house before Billy had time to wonder why she hadn't spoken to him, not a single word.

He started across the street, waited for a car to pass, and then walked up his own sidewalk, turning at the front steps to see if the girl had come back, but she hadn't. It was no fun hanging out here alone. He couldn't think of anywhere else to go, so he went inside, where his mom, Chris, was still sleeping. A white bolt of envy crossed his chest at the thought of her sleeping, without a care in the world, while Dad . . . but he didn't want to think about him. About how, when Dad had packed his things, he'd taken all five bottles out of the bottom cupboard and folded them gently in clothes at the top of his suitcase.

"Go ahead, Zak, drink yourself to death. See if I care!"

Mom had yelled with that sharp sound in her voice, as if she were slicing something.

Billy closed his eyes against the memory. He didn't want to think about Dad, and where he might be going, and when he might come back. He shoved the Typhoon into his pocket and went into the building. He needed to find that book, the one with the tricks that Mom and Dad had given him for his eleventh birthday.

He'd really wanted roller blades for his birthday, and a skateboard, and one of those new water guns that had lots of space in its tank, but he hadn't gotten any of these things. The yo-yo was pretty fun, though. He liked it after he'd opened the package, and tried not to think about the other stuff. He especially liked that it was called a "Typhoon." In grade five they'd studied natural disasters, and the tropical cyclone was one of Billy's favorites. He sometimes felt as if he had a real typhoon inside him, making him jump around and do other crazy stuff.

There were twenty-one yo-yo tricks in the book. Billy could do more than half of them. He planned to learn them all. All twenty-one of them. Then he and Dad were going to go to the talent contest at the park. Billy wanted to think about winning but he pushed it out of his mind. If you wanted something too much, you screwed it up. Wrecked your chances. He knew that better than anyone.

"If I don't see you in the future, I'll see you in the pasture," Dad had called out on his way down the hall. What did that mean? Did it mean Dad would be back in time for the contest? He'd promised Billy he was going to come, but now Billy wasn't so sure. He crossed his fingers. Please let him come back, he thought.

As Billy opened the door to their apartment, he listened. Nothing stirred: the kitchen and living room were quiet, and his own bedroom and the one where his mother slept were silent and still. If Dad were home, he'd have the radio on and be singing along and frying something— bacon, or mushrooms. Mushrooms in lots of butter. Billy couldn't smell anything now except yesterday's garbage.

Billy walked down the hall past the kitchen and headed into his own room. He didn't feel like going back to bed. He didn't feel like doing anything, but he was too restless to keep still. He felt as though inside him a storm was breaking free, ready to spill out and dislodge anything in its path.

Chapter Two

Already the sun was like an iron, pressing against the thin curtain on Billy's bedroom window. It didn't matter so much if school days were warm, because you got to spend the hottest part of them inside where the rooms were air-conditioned. But now, when the apartment was like an oven, there was nowhere to go. Nowhere that didn't cost money, and Billy knew better than to ask Mom for any money right now.

He flopped onto his bed and looked up at the ceiling. The crack across the middle grinned down at him like a jack-o'-lantern. What had his teacher called those lines in the earth? He thought for a minute and remembered. *Fault lines.* What if this was actually a fault line, and the halves of ceiling were rubbing against each other until all at once, there'd be an earthquake and the ceiling would open up like a split pumpkin? *"Look out, it's gonna explode!"* he cried, watching the ceiling for any possibility of action. But nothing happened.

After a while, he picked up a penny from his floor and pressed it hard against the back of his hand. When he removed it, there was a white spot on his skin where the penny had been.

Mrs. Schmidt, their neighbor, said that pennies were good luck. Sometimes when he went over there, she gave him one and told him to make a wish. Now he held the penny in his palm and closed his eyes. "I hope I win the contest," he said, trying to sound as if he didn't much care one way or the other. Then he tossed the penny onto his bed and headed out to the kitchen to get some cereal. He stood, spooning cereal into his mouth with one hand, while the other hand kept the yo-yo in motion.

"You should sit down to eat," Mom said as she came into the kitchen, her voice all crackly and tired. Billy hardly ever sat down when he ate. His body felt uncomfortable when he tried to be still and he often imagined that from the inside his bones were sharp as lightning, electrifying his skin.

"Here's your morning pill," she said, handing it to him. He took one small white pill in the morning and another at noon. Sometimes the prescription ran out, and if he went to school the teacher phoned home and complained that he was too hyper to work, but now there were lots of pills in the bottle. He shoved the pill into his mouth and got a drink at the tap.

"Well, you save on dishes that way." Mom laughed, and then sighed, rubbing her big belly where the baby was.

"Maybe you should go to the pool," she told Billy. "It's gonna be hot. And I don't want you here alone all day."

"Watch this," said Billy. He cast the yo-yo, then twisted the string in front of his face, making a figure X. "*Tiger at the Zoo*, it's called," he said, with his face behind the X. "See? I'm the tiger!"

His mother nodded, then put down her glass and looked at the clock.

"I gotta be at work soon. You can walk with me if you wanna swim. Bring a clean towel. And when you come back, stop at the Schmidts' place."

Billy threw on his trunks and shoved a towel into a plastic bag, and then went outside into the hallway to wait for his mother. Chris. Her real name was Chrysta Lee, but she'd shortened it. Just like Dad's name was Zachary, but everyone called him Zak. Billy knew he himself had a longer name, but just now he couldn't remember what it was. Sometimes he filed things in his brain and couldn't find them when he needed them.

Mrs. Schmidt was cooking those Dutch pancakes; he could tell from the smell of hot butter that wafted out from under her door. Maybe she'd give him some, if there were any leftovers after Mr. Schmidt had finished eating. Mrs. Schmidt had a funny name for her husband. "Pork Chop," she called him.

"I got Pork Chop new slippers today," she'd say, or, if she were visiting with Mom, "I wonder how Pork Chop is doing? Maybe I'd better go check on him."

Billy knew Mr. Schmidt was sick, but he thought that for a sick person, he ate pretty good. At least, Mrs. Schmidt always seemed to be feeding him.

In the stuffy hallway, Billy felt as if lava was running through his veins. He brushed at his arms and wondered if everyone felt as if they had a natural disaster inside. When Mom joined him, he thought she looked flushed. Maybe she was feeling the same way he was.

"Do you ever feel like there's a volcano inside you just waiting to erupt?" Billy asked. "Or a cyclone, or a flood? Or maybe lightning and thunder?"

"Hurry up," she said, pushing him into the elevator. "I'd just better be on time for work, that's all."

The pool was in the Tropical Paradise Hotel. His mom worked there cleaning rooms, so Billy was allowed to swim whenever he liked. If you could call it swimming. The pool was so small that Billy could cross it in three strokes, but it was deep enough for a water slide. It was the only water slide in town.

Today, as he climbed the stairs to the top of the slide, he wondered what the pool had looked like when it was new. Probably a lot nicer. Now it had so many rust marks along the sides that the water looked brown instead of blue, and the painted cement walls above the water seemed to be shedding their skin.

What if the walls really were made of snakeskin, and underneath there was a snake? Billy smiled at the idea as he reached the last step. Then he looked at his reflection in the mirror that covered the wall. His dark hair stuck up like clumps of playground grass, his eyes were far apart and slightly slanted, and his body was so skinny that his ribs made his chest look like a set of monkey bars.

"I should lift weights," he thought, but you had to be sixteen to get into the weight room. Five more years.

A white scar ran down the middle of his chest from the surgery to repair the hole in his heart. He'd been born with the hole, and when he was five, the doctors had fixed it. He didn't remember much about being in the hospital. It had been a long time ago.

There was a sign at the top of the slide, but Billy couldn't read any of the words. He named a few of the letters: P-O-O-L R-U-L-E-S. Then he lifted himself into the mouth of the slide and pushed off, leaning backward to pick up speed, and raising his spine so that only his heels and the back of his head were touching the slide.

"Here I come!" His voice sounded as though he were yelling into a paper towel tube.

He splashed off the bottom of the slide and treaded water for a minute. Good thing the pool was empty. There wasn't really room here for more than one person.

He practiced floating on his back, trying not to think about the talent contest but thinking about it anyway, like you poke your tongue into a loose tooth that's not quite ready to come out. The prize was twenty-five bucks. He had never had that much money, not ever, and he thought about what he'd do with it, how he'd spend some of it on candy, and some of it on one of those new water guns they had at the store.

He went down the slide a few more times and then pushed himself around the bottom of the pool, eyes open, counting to see how many seconds he could hold his breath. It was easy for the first ten seconds. Then it got hard. Then easier again. Then really hard. His lungs burned. Forty-three. Forty-four. Forty-five seconds. He burst up to the surface, his chest on fire.

For a minute he couldn't remember what he was doing. The sensation of the pool around him evaporated, and he stood dizzily looking up at the top of the slide, where the mirror reflected the light from a window. It's the moon, he thought. Then he shook his head. Of course it wasn't the moon. How could the moon be inside a building? How could the moon be inside anything?

Suddenly he could hear voices from the change room. Other people were coming.

Without taking time to think, he climbed out of the pool and scrambled up the steps of the slide. By the time he got to the top, the newcomers were on the stairs below. Billy pushed himself off and slid until he got to the middle, where he pressed his hands and feet against opposite walls and lifted his body into a sort of bridge. In a few minutes, a kid came barreling under him.

"Hey!" the kid yelled.

Billy stayed where he was and soon the next kid was coming down.

"Whadya think you're doing!" she screeched, sliding under Billy with just inches to spare.

Suddenly, one of Billy's feet slipped and he fell. Bang! Someone hit him from behind and then pushed him, their bodies connected as they hit the water. He struggled to the surface, spitting out blood from biting his tongue.

"Hey, kid, what's the matter with you? Don't you know the rules?" The man who had crashed into him spoke angrily, pushing his long dark hair out of his eyes and reaching a tattooed arm for the side of the pool. "What are you doing in here alone, anyway? I bet you just walked in off the street!"

Billy lifted himself out of the pool and fumbled in his bag for the towel.

"Some of us are paying guests, you know!" called the man.

Billy thought about explaining that his mom worked here, but sometimes it just wasn't worth it. As he pulled out the towel and dried his face, one of the kids giggled, the laughter nipping at Billy like a stray dog. What's so funny? he thought as he tried to tie the towel around his waist, and then, giving up, headed for the change room with more laughter following him. The towel seemed unusually small.

Suddenly Billy knew why the kids were laughing, and his face burned. Instead of a swimming towel, he'd brought one of Mom's checkered dishtowels. He threw it on the floor and ducked into the change room. Let them laugh. I don't care, he thought to himself. But deep down, he knew he did care.

"Why am I so stupid?" he muttered as the hot water beat down on him from the shower, the drops sharp as hail against his bare back.

At school it seemed that everything he did proved how dumb he was. Some of the other kids, like Eddie Mundy, were quick to notice his mistakes. Like the time he'd tried to clean the chalk brushes in the big metal milk dispenser in the front hallway. It looked a lot like the brush cleaner, which was kept around the corner. Probably the milk machine had the word "Milk" on it somewhere, but since Billy couldn't read it didn't much matter what words were on it.

Billy could read a few words, but it wasn't real reading. He knew the words on the cards that the teacher assistant held up for him to practice. Days of the week. Months of the year. *The. And. Because. Then.* Meaningless words that by themselves weren't any use at all.

When his class read from their novel, he tried to turn the pages and keep up, but sometimes he got off track and realized that everybody else was way ahead of him. He hated that feeling, that breathless, panicky feeling, as if he was at the bottom of the pool, counting to fifty.

His dad had tried to work with him at home. Billy remembered with shame the way Dad had said, "Come on, Billy, you've got to pay attention! You'll never amount to anything if you can't learn to read." And Billy had tried to pay attention. The trouble was that no matter how hard he tried, something inside his head just wouldn't co-operate.

"Loser!" Eddie Mundy would whisper on his way past Billy's desk. "Reading baby words. Must be a baby, eh? Does Baby Billy wear a diaper, too?"

Sometimes, the other kids would write notes about him. Billy knew this because he'd find them sometimes, small scraps of paper with his name on them, but he couldn't read what they said. He just knew they said bad things.

I've got to win that contest, Billy told himself, gulping deep breaths as he turned off the shower and dried himself with his T-shirt. That'll show 'em. If I win that contest, that'll show 'em all!

Chapter Three

Instead of unlocking the door to his apartment, Billy stood outside Mrs. Schmidt's door and sniffed. Dutch pancakes. You could still smell them. She made good ones, with crispy edges. It was the potatoes in them that made them so tender. And the outsides were crunchy because she always let lots of butter melt in the pan before she cooked them.

Suddenly the door opened and Mrs. Schmidt stood in the entrance, a pink apron over her flowered housedress and her hair up in curlers.

"Billy!" she said with a smile. "I thought I heard the elevator! Your mom called earlier and said you'd be along. Come on in, won't you? I've got some pancakes I need you to take care of for me."

"Okay," said Billy. "Sure!" He trailed her into the kitchen, sniffing at the warm aroma of pancakes and the underlying smell of lemons that always hung there.

When Billy had first met Gladys Schmidt, he'd thought she looked like a pig, her broad, age-spotted face as pink as skin could be. She even had bristles on her chin and a pink nose with the end sort of pushed in. It was funny she looked like a pig, because she collected pigs—china pigs, glass pigs, pottery pigs, even cloth pigs. The apartment was full of pigs.

Mrs. Schmidt served Billy a big plateful of pancakes while he sat at the kitchen table and traced his finger around the plastic tulips on the cloth. He always sat down at Mrs. Schmidt's to eat, because he knew it wasn't proper to stand. He crossed and uncrossed his legs, trying to fight off the restlessness, and picked up the pig salt and pepper shakers, even though he wasn't going to use them.

He thought of Mrs. Schmidt's first name. Gladys. It wasn't short for anything. Just like Mrs. Schmidt herself, who wasn't short at all.

"What's doing with you?" Mrs. Schmidt asked as she set two kinds of syrup on the table: blueberry and maple. "Any girlfriends yet?"

Billy blushed and stared hard at the salt and pepper shakers, a white pig and a black pig, thinking of the girl across the street. Could Mrs. Schmidt have seen him talking to her?

"There's that pretty girl across the road," Mrs. Schmidt went on, as if reading his mind. "The quiet one. She's from Romania, you know, one of them adopted kids. I heard that the orphanage there treated them real bad, so she's lucky that couple went and got her a few years ago. They moved here from Saskatoon in the winter. He bought a car dealership downtown. The North Battleford Motors. Lucky this place is big enough to support four dealerships. I heard the Motors is doing pretty well."

Billy nodded politely and poured the syrup. He put blueberry on the bottom ones, and then maple on the others. Finally, he spread some whipped cream on the very top, from a blue bowl that Mrs. Schmidt put in front of him.

He ate until he couldn't hold another bite, and he could tell by Mrs. Schmidt's expression that she was pleased with him.

"Thanks for that," she told him, pressing a penny into his hand. "For luck!"

"You're welcome," said Billy, slipping the penny into his pocket. "I'll make a wish later, okay?"

"I didn't know what I was going to do with all those pancakes," Mrs. Schmidt went on. "My Pork Chop can't eat like he used to do, bless his soul."

As Billy went out, he caught a glimpse of Mr. Schmidt asleep in an easy chair in the living room, his feet resting on a pink wooden pig. What a life, he thought, enviously. Pancakes, probably all the time!

The hallway was empty; the other tenants were away. Probably on holiday at the lake. Billy wished he'd be going to the lake this summer, but it didn't look likely. Not with Mom working all the time.

"Come back anytime," called Mrs. Schmidt. "We're always here."

The apartment seemed extra quiet when he walked in. He wandered into the living room and stared at his dad's guitar, still propped in the corner. Dad kept it there, out of the way, because he didn't have a case for it. Billy's heart lifted. Dad would never leave his guitar. Not for good. For sure he'd be back!

Billy jumped as the fridge started to hum and realized he'd been holding his breath. He went into his bedroom and took out his yo-yo. The trick book was propped on his bedside table, and he tried to follow the diagrams to learn some of the new routines. He couldn't read their names, so he just made up his own. *Moon Shadow. Water Slider. Pancake Flip.*

After a while, he looked out the window and saw the girl again, sitting on her steps, as before. It would be a couple of hours until Mom got home from work. He might as well go across the street, see what the girl was up to.

• • •

"What are you so dressed up for?" he asked as he went up the front walk, staring at her white lacy dress and matching purse.

The girl just shrugged her shoulders. She was drawing in her notebook, and when Billy looked, he could see a building and beside it, the figure of a person. The girl spread her fingers over the drawing, so Billy couldn't see the details.

"Come on!" he said. "Lemme see!"

The girl shook her head.

"Please? I won't hurt anything. And I won't laugh." He knew how awful it was to be laughed at.

The girl looked at Billy for a long moment. Then she

slowly moved her hand away. Billy saw that she'd sketched a box beside the front door of the building.

"What's that doll doing in the box?" he asked. The girl shook her head.

"I don't understand," said Billy. "Is it a doll?"

The girl shook her head again, pointed to herself, and kept on drawing.

"It's you? It's you as a baby?" he asked. When she nodded, he sat down beside her and watched her draw.

"Hush little baby, don't say a word," he burst out singing. "Mama's gonna buy you a mockingbird."

The girl looked at him for a moment and he saw that fleeting smile again. Then she went back to drawing.

"My mom's having a baby, but not for a few months," he said. The girl didn't answer.

"That's a church," he said, when she had finished the building. "I can tell by the steeple." He paused, then went on. "What are you doing in the box? And who's that man beside you?"

The girl scowled up at him.

"It isn't a man?" Billy guessed. The girl shook her head. "Okay, it's a girl," Billy went on. "Is it your mom?"

The girl looked up at him intently, as if measuring him in some way, and nodded. Then she drew a big moon in the sky beside the steeple and used a yellow pastel to cast moonlight down on the church and the baby and the mother.

"Is your mom taking you to church?" Billy asked. "Is that it? For a midnight service?" He knew about those, because sometimes Mrs. Schmidt went to church at night and took his mother along.

The girl shook her head and glanced up at Billy before she started putting away her crayons. She had the longest eyelashes of anyone he'd ever seen, and Billy saw suddenly that her eyes were full of tears. He took another look. What was the matter with her?

"Natasha, come in for lunch," called a voice at the window.

"Don't cry. It's okay, really," said Billy, jumping to his feet. "Does she give you a bad lunch, is that it? Like carrots? Or cabbage? Or oatmeal?"

The girl shook her head. The ghost of a smile appeared again, then vanished.

"Hey, do you know about the talent contest?" Billy asked. "It's next Thursday. I'm going to win, and my dad is going to come."

Billy hoped this last statement was true and, to make sure it was, he said it again.

"My dad is going to come, you know."

The girl tilted her small face towards the sky. Billy remembered how she had stared at the moon that morning. He looked up, following her gaze, but all he saw was blue sky.

"There's no moon there," he said. "Why are you always looking for the moon?"

The girl turned and went inside before he could think of anything else to say. The big front windows, with their closed curtains, loomed over him and, above them, two other windows stared down at him like dark eyes. He turned. No use hanging around here any longer.

Chapter Four

The next day was Saturday. Billy heard his mother getting ready for work and he lay in bed, listening to the moths purr against his window. Somehow in the night they always got inside the screen. He watched them drowsily for a minute, their paper thin wings, their quick, desperate attempts to locate an escape route, and then he went over and lifted the window, just enough, and gently pushed them all out, one after the other. One by one, they beat against the fresh air and then disappeared into the morning, lifting something inside him with their wings.

Billy looked at the calendar on his wall. There was a big star around today's date—Saturday, July fifteenth. Today was going to be a good day. Today was the day they were going to the circus.

Billy loved the circus. He loved the sounds, the colors, the smells. He loved the acts, and how you could watch more than one thing at once. There'd be someone balancing on a trapeze, and next to that a dozen dogs getting out of a Volkswagen, and next to that a circle of elephants. He also loved the food. Corn on the cob, snow cones, candy apples. He especially loved the candy apples. He rolled over in bed and imagined their sweet scent, and then how it felt to bite through the hard red coating to the tangy apple underneath.

"Billy, I'm going now," called his mother. "Are you awake?"

"Uh-huh," said Billy. "What time is the circus?"

She came into his room and sat on the end of his bed.

"Honey, I forgot all about it. I picked up an extra shift today and then I've got my AA meeting, so I'm not sure what we're gonna do. Plus your dad has the tickets . . ." her voice trailed off. It came back to Billy in a flash that because Dad was gone, so was the circus.

"Where is he?" Billy said. "Can I call him? I could remind him about the circus . . ."

"Never mind," said his mother. "There'll be other circuses." Her voice was silvery sharp. "We can get along just fine without him. You'll have to miss the circus today, but that's okay. I'll try and bring a treat home later." She's slicing the circus off today, Billy thought, gripping the bedsheet in his hands. It isn't fair!

A treat. Mom thinks a treat can make up for missing the circus. His mouth was still watering at the thought of the candy apples. And he'd miss all the other food and the circus acts. How could Mom trade him one treat for all that?

"Okay?" said his mother, but she wasn't really asking. She stood up and looked at him for a moment, her eyes widening as if she wanted to say something more, but then she turned. "Be good," she called over her shoulder. "Remember, I'll have to feed you oatmeal if you forget to eat today." Neither of them smiled at this, although she often said it as a joke. Then she left the apartment.

Billy bounced on his bed for a while, but that was no fun. He wished he had a trampoline. He wished he had roller blades, too. Maybe Mom would bring him roller blades tonight, for the treat.

If he'd gotten roller blades for his birthday, he could use them right now. Slide his feet in, go cruising down the sidewalk, faster than he could run. Dad had promised him roller blades but must have forgotten, like his parents forgot a lot of things. Billy sighed and looked at the trick book. He practiced a few new ones, thinking about the contest on Thursday and trying not to imagine the worst. What if Dad didn't come home? Of course he would . . . but what if he didn't?

Maybe Billy could go to the contest by himself. The idea crossed his mind carefully, with small jerky steps, and he turned the yo-yo around and around in his hands, considering. Maybe he could go to the contest, and Dad would meet him there. Maybe that's what Dad had been planning all along. Billy would go to the contest, and Dad would be there ready to play and sing while Billy did his tricks. Dad would have to come back home first and get the guitar, though. He never sang without it.

Billy tried a few tricks and then examined the string on the Typhoon. No knots. But you never knew when knots would appear. What if he was in the middle of his routine and something happened? What if he forgot a trick, or the string knotted or even broke? At least if Dad were there, he'd help him figure out what to do. But if Billy were by himself, and something happened . . . the thought made him feel sick to his stomach. He felt a cyclone gathering in the middle of his belly, and swallowed hard. Think of something else, he told himself. Anything else. He flipped open the trick book and practiced one of the tricks. Of course, Dad would be there. He'd promised, hadn't he?

Suddenly Billy remembered he was supposed to eat breakfast. He ran out to the kitchen and took his pill, gulping water from the tap. Then he had some cereal and walked around the apartment, the threadbare carpet rough against his bare feet. He stopped in front of the guitar. It was made of caramel-colored wood, and there was a silver panel on the front, running along beside the strings. Billy crouched down and breathed on the panel, and then shone it with his T-shirt until he could see his face reflected in it. Then he stood up and looked out the window. The girl was on her steps.

Billy went downstairs on the elevator and ran across the street.

"What are you doing?" he called, running into her yard and doing a cartwheel on the grass. "Natasha, that's your name, right? Can I see?"

The girl looked at him for a moment, and then continued drawing. He did another cartwheel, and another. Then he went and stood beside her. She was still working on the picture from yesterday, the one with the baby in the box.

This time she didn't cover it up with her hand.

"You like looking at the moon, don't you?" he asked. She nodded.

"My teacher told us a story about how the moon got into the sky," said Billy. "Did your teacher tell you that one?"

The girl shook her head and kept drawing.

"It's the story about Raven, and how she stole the moon from a woman who kept it in a box in her house. The moon was supposed to be a secret, but Raven discovered it."

The girl drew some more.

"Are you sure your teacher never told you this one?" Billy asked. "Raven stole the moon from the woman and tried to keep it a secret from everybody, but it was too heavy for her and she couldn't hang onto it anymore. So she let it go in the sky."

The girl didn't answer.

"You draw good," Billy said. "I wish I could draw. I can't. I can just do yo-yo tricks. Wanna see?"

The girl nodded again and Billy took out the Typhoon. He tried a few tricks and then looked at her. She was looking interested, her small white teeth biting her bottom lip, and when he finished, she clapped her hands.

"You like that? You want to see more?" He tried a few other tricks and she clapped again. He felt on top of the world.

"I'm learning new ones all the time. I'm gonna be as good as it gets and I'm gonna win that contest," Billy said. "With my dad. Except that my dad isn't here right now.

He's—" Billy tried to think of something to say that would make sense, but couldn't think of anything. "—He's just gone, I guess," he said, finally. "I don't know where." He swallowed hard.

Suddenly the happiness he'd felt a minute ago slid out from under him. Something grabbed his insides and pulled until his chest hurt. He felt as if a sound was going to come from there, from his chest, or maybe his heart where the hole had been, and so he spoke quickly to stop any other sound from coming out.

"He's just gone. And I don't know if he's coming back," he said.

The words surprised him but they didn't seem to surprise the girl. She looked at him for a minute, and then picked up her crayon and started drawing some more on her picture. She filled in the dress of the mother with blue and then made the baby's gown yellow.

As Billy watched, she folded a crease in the paper and then tore off the part with the mother on it, which she put into her purse.

"What did you do that for?" he asked. "You ruined it!"

The girl looked at the sky, and then took the mother out of her purse, laying her down near the baby. Then she looked at Billy as if to say, "You see?"

"First the mother went away, and then she came back?" Billy guessed. "She came back to see the baby?"

The girl nodded. For a minute, Billy didn't speak. Then he asked, "You think my dad'll do that? Come back to see me?"

The girl nodded again.

"Well, he'll have to," said Billy. "Because he's coming back for the contest, that's for sure."

The girl started putting away her crayons.

"Did your mother leave you?" asked Billy, the idea rising in his mind like a flash flood. "She left you there, at the church, when you were a baby?"

The girl looked at him for a minute, considering. Then she nodded.

"I get it," said Billy. "And then the church people took you to the orphanage, and then Mr. and Mrs. Arnold came and got you. A few years ago, Mrs. Schmidt said."

The girl looked at Billy with the same expression he'd seen yesterday, her eyes glistening as if she were going to cry.

"But your mother used to come back," said Billy, thinking of his dad. "She came back to see you."

Natasha put her fingers to her lips.

"Shshsh," he interpreted. "It's a secret. It's a secret that your mother came back to visit you?"

Natasha blinked and closed her crayon box.

"It's okay," he said. "You're in a good place, now. Not like that old orphanage." He stopped. He couldn't remember what Mrs. Schmidt had said about the orphanage. "Where it wasn't very nice," he added.

The girl shook her head and a strangled noise came out of her that sounded to Billy as if it might have come from his own throat.

"Natasha, it's dinnertime," called a voice from the house.

"So your name really is Natasha," said Billy quickly, to push down the sadness that was still brimming up inside. When the girl didn't respond, he said, "It's a nice name. Better than my one, *Billy*. Lots of people are named Billy. But I don't know any other Natashas. Do you? Do you know any others?"

Natasha didn't look at him but she pointed at the woman she'd drawn.

"Your mother," Billy guessed as she stood up and went into the house. "Your mother's name is Natasha, too!"

The screen door banged behind her and Billy was left alone on the front steps.

"My mother's name is Chris," he called, "for Chrysta Lee. And my dad's called Zak. For Zachary. My name is short for something too, but I can't remember it." He took a deep breath and waited.

Nobody answered.

Billy hoped his mother wouldn't leave their baby anywhere in a box after it was born. She sometimes went to church with Mrs. Schmidt when she wasn't going to work or to one of her meetings, but she probably wouldn't leave the baby at church. He imagined you could leave a baby anywhere, though. If you wanted to.

He thought about Natasha's mother leaving her and felt sorry for Natasha until he thought about his father and realized that it was just the same. Dad had left him, just like Natasha's mother had left her.

Suddenly he felt so bad that he wanted to cry. Instead, he brushed his hands on his shorts and headed down the walk and across the street, dodging a car that had come zooming around the corner. He'd just learn some more of those yo-yo tricks, that's what he'd do. Dad wouldn't leave behind a champion yo-yo master, that was for sure. And he only had five days until the contest, until Dad would be back.

As Billy walked up his front steps, he clapped his hand to his forehead, and turned, triumphantly.

"William!" he called out. "Billy is short for William!"

Nothing moved on the hot summer street except that, in an instant, the wind came up and pushed some elm seeds from the gutter into a whirlpool on the dry asphalt. A few clouds came skidding across the sky and Billy looked at them, wondering if there would be rain. They were white ones, though. You never got rain from those. In a few minutes, the wind had blown itself out and the street was still again. Billy turned and went inside.

Chapter Five

"Help me with these dishes and then run to the store for some Cheez Whiz," said Billy's mother on Sunday morning. "We're all out and I've got a craving coming on."

Billy picked up a dishtowel and rubbed at one of the cups from the draining board. "Mom, you wouldn't leave your baby anywhere after it's born, would you?" he asked suddenly.

"Leave the baby? Of course not!" she said, turning to look at him. "What makes you ask that?"

"I just know a girl whose mom left her somewhere once," Billy said. "But you wouldn't, would you?"

"Of course not, and I wouldn't leave you, either. Just because your dad left doesn't mean anyone else's gonna leave. You and me, we're a team. Remember what that means?"

"Yeah," said Billy.

"What?" his mother prompted.

"It means we stick together. Like a basketball team."

"Right," said his mother. "I used to be pretty good at

basketball, once upon a time. You'd never know it now," she went on, looking down at her big belly. "But I used to be good."

"Even if the baby's stupid like me, you won't ever leave it?" Billy remembered taking the dishtowel to the pool, and his face felt hot.

"You're not stupid, and don't you say that," said his mother, pulling the plug in the sink. Billy flung the towel on the shelf. "Remember what Gladys Schmidt says? 'All God's creatures have a place in the choir,'" his mom said. "Means everyone's different, and that's okay. Don't you forget that, Billy. Now, how about going to the store for me?"

"I thought you were supposed to want ice cream all the time when you're pregnant," Billy said hopefully.

"Nope, not with this one. Cheez Whiz. With you, I wanted tomatoes. Tomato soup, tomato juice, canned tomatoes . . ."

"Canned tomatoes—gross!" said Billy.

"Should have called you *Tom*," said his mother. "Get it, *Tom*ato?"

Billy laughed and put on his shoes. They were a little too big, but Mom had said he'd grow into them. It wasn't until he got to the store that he realized he'd put the shoes on the wrong feet. He stopped outside the door and switched them, but not before somebody noticed.

Eddie Mundy had been lounging against the store window. He snickered as Billy changed his shoes.

"Oh, doesn't the little baby know which shoe goes on

which foot?" Eddie sneered. "Baby needs his mommy to help him put his shoes on."

"I'm not a baby," said Billy through clenched teeth.

"You are if I say you are," said Eddie, giving him a push.

He'd like to smack that Eddie, always picking on him. First at school, and now here. He'd like to pound the meanness right out of him, once and for all, but instead Billy darted past him into the store.

Coolness from the store's air conditioner made goose bumps rise on his skin. He shivered and hurried to the dairy aisle to look for the Cheez Whiz.

He found it easily enough, but there were two kinds of jars. Which one did Mom want? One had something written in blue letters above the brand name, and he wondered if maybe it said "Sale." But why would they have both jars side by side on the shelf, if one was on sale, and the other wasn't? It didn't make sense. He picked up both jars to look at them more closely.

An older man was nearby getting eggs, and Billy said, "Excuse me?"

"What?" said the man, crossly.

"What's the difference here between these two kinds?" asked Billy. "Do you know?"

"The one in your left hand is the *light* brand," snapped the man. "Can't you read?" He turned away and Billy heard him muttering. "You kids are all the same, trying to get into trouble."

"I'm not trying to get into trouble—" Billy started, but

the man had already gone. Billy reached up and put the jar back on the shelf, but it slipped off and fell, hitting the floor with a crash that sounded like thunder. He could see the glass had cracked. Quickly, he stuffed the jar back where it belonged and walked away, hoping nobody else had seen.

"I'm a natural disaster waiting to happen," Billy muttered, darting towards the checkout.

It was while he was waiting there that he heard the two girls talking. He recognized them from school, although they were a year older.

"Good thing you got your name in on Friday," one was saying. "Because the deadline's tomorrow, right?" She pointed to a poster over on the bulletin board. "That's just like the poster they used last year, except they've changed the dates."

"Yeah," said the other. "I wonder how many kids are entering. Samantha said nobody else was doing Irish dancing."

"You're a good dancer, Maya," the first girl said. "I bet you'll win the talent contest for sure."

"I hope so," said Maya. "I could really use that twenty-five bucks."

• • •

Early Monday morning, Billy walked determinedly down the sidewalk towards the park. Good thing he'd heard those girls talking or he wouldn't have known today was the deadline for entering his name! He listened to a lawnmower buzzing the grass behind one of the big houses near Natasha's, and at the same time he tried not to step on any cracks in the pavement. The lukewarm cement tickled his bare toes. *Step on a crack, break your mother's back.* The muscles in his wrists ached from practicing the yo-yo tricks. He'd been working hard, using every spare minute, and now he could do fifteen tricks. Sixteen, if he could get the next one right. He called it *The CN Tower* and it was really hard.

Suddenly, he realized someone was following him. He turned around. It was Natasha. She was carrying the yellow notebook.

"Hey, Natasha, what are you doing? I'm going to the park—do you wanna come?" Billy asked.

Natasha walked beside him for a few steps.

"How come you never talk?" he asked. "Can you talk?" The girl shrugged. Then a voice called from behind them.

"Natasha, it's almost time to get ready! Remember, you have a doctor's appointment today."

The girl turned, looked back at Billy, and then started towards Mrs. Arnold who was standing in front of their hedge.

"Why are you going to the doctor?" called Billy. "Are you sick?" Natasha gave a quick shake of the head, and then broke into a run. She was so light on her feet that Billy thought she was almost flying. Billy watched Natasha and her mother disappear along the sidewalk through the hedge, and then turned back towards the park. He hoped that if Natasha was sick, he wasn't going to catch it. When he got sick his nose plugged up and it seemed to last forever.

The park was bordered by beds of red and white flowers. Petunias, Billy thought they were called, and he breathed in their thick dusty scent and sneezed. When he opened the park gate, he saw Eddie Mundy sitting against a tree, swatting at mosquitoes.

"Hey, are you gonna register for the contest?" asked Eddie. He took hold of a spot on his arm where a mosquito had started to suck and squeezed until the insect popped.

"Yeah. What about it?" said Billy, staring at the speckled blood on Eddie's arm.

"Well, you'd better hurry. You're late. Give me the five bucks entry fee, and then get over to the registration table as fast as you can." Eddie brushed a thumb across his arm, leaving a red smudge.

"What?" said Billy, uncertainly.

"You heard me, Chinaman. Five bucks, paid to me, before you enter the contest."

"I'm not Chinese," said Billy. Kids often thought he was Chinese because of his eyes, but he wasn't. He knew for sure he wasn't, because neither of his parents was Chinese, and you had to have at least one parent who was. He reached inside his pocket but all he found was one of Mrs. Schmidt's pennies.

"Maybe you are a Chinaman and maybe you aren't," said Eddie. "But you owe me five bucks."

"Wait—can I run home and get it?" asked Billy. "Will I have time before they finish entering people?" Maybe

Eddie would give him a break this time.

"If you run all the way there and all the way back," said Eddie, "you might just make it. I'll tell them to wait for you, but they won't be able to wait for long." He had a funny look on his face.

"Thanks!" said Billy, turning and breaking into a run. Maybe Eddie wasn't so bad after all. "Thanks! I'll be right back!" he called. Eddie didn't answer.

Billy felt a surge of power in his arms and legs. He knew he could do it. He had to do it! After a few blocks, his bare heels throbbed from pounding against the cement and he had a bloody cut on one toe, but he kept on running. He ran as fast as he could, all the way home, only stopping once to breathe deeply the smell of cut grass in front of the neighbor's yard. The elevator was too slow, so he took the stairs, all three flights, and at the top he stopped for just a minute to catch his breath, hoping that he was fast enough.

It was quiet in the apartment. He took a few shaky steps inside and then stopped, a twister starting in the pit of his stomach. Where was he going to get the money? Mom was at work and Dad was gone. Where would he get five dollars? He didn't have any money of his own. He rubbed his sore toe against the top of the other foot and left a red streak on the skin. Then he went into the kitchen.

Some of the change from the Cheez Whiz still lay on the kitchen counter. He looked at it, hopefully, but although he couldn't figure out the exact amount, it was only nickels and dimes, not nearly five dollars' worth.

He wiped the sweat from his forehead with one hand, and looked around the room. What should he do? He could ask Mrs. Schmidt for money, but he knew Mom wouldn't like it. Begging for handouts, she'd call it. He had to do something. He had to have that money!

Suddenly he saw his mother's purse hanging on the hook. She didn't take it to work because she was afraid someone would break into her locker and steal it. "No good tempting fate," was what she said.

There might be money in the purse! He quickly opened it and pulled out her wallet. Inside there was a five-dollar bill and some change. He took out the five. This is my lucky day, he thought.

He ran back to the park as fast as he could and his knees trembled a bit when he saw Eddie at the gate.

"Am I on time?" he said, his lips sticky from the effort it took to breathe. "Have I missed it? Are they still there?"

Eddie reached out his hand and Billy dropped the money onto his palm.

"I put in a good word for you, kid. They're waiting over by the paddling pool. Go ahead."

Billy brushed his hand across his mouth and started over toward the pool.

"And don't tell them about the money," Eddie said, with a grin. "I'm going to . . . um . . . surprise them later, when I've finished collecting. Like, when I've finished collecting from everyone."

Billy hurried over to the table that had been set up for registration. Samantha Peeteetuce, a girl who used to babysit him when he was younger, was handing out the forms.

"Hi, Billy," she said. "Did you see our poster? Are you going to enter the contest?"

"Yeah," he said. "I'm going to do yo-yo tricks."

"Yo-yo tricks! Well, that'll be great!" she said. "We don't have any other acts like that. Please fill out this form so we'll have all the information about your performance."

Billy's eyes swam as he looked at the form. He couldn't make out any of the words, although he guessed the blank at the top was for his name. BILLY RAY, he printed in big letters on the line, and then looked desperately at the other spaces.

"I don't think you'll need any of this other stuff," he said to Samantha. "My routine is pretty simple. I'll just be standing there doing some tricks. Maybe twenty-one of them, if I can learn them all in time. I already know fifteen real good."

"Fifteen tricks!" said Samantha. "That's really good, Billy, and twenty-one would be amazing! But we have to have a title for your act."

"You write it," said Billy, shoving the paper at her. "I don't print too good. It'll be called . . ." he thought feverishly for a moment, wondering what name to give his act. Billy and his yo-yo? Yo-yo Billy? These names didn't sound right, and he looked around, hoping for another idea.

"I know!" he said, suddenly. "It'll be called: Billy Ray—the Amazing Yo-yo Master."

"Well, I need your age, too," said Samantha, putting the title of the act on the paper.

"Eleven."

"And your address?"

"Come on," said Billy, starting to panic. He never could seem to remember his address, no matter how many times he practiced it. Some things just wouldn't stay in his head.

"You don't really need all that," he said, looking back at the other kids behind him who had come to register. "How about just my phone number?"

"Okay, that should be all right," said Samantha. Billy carefully told her the number and she wrote it down.

"There," she said. "Now, who is your sponsor?"

"My what?" asked Billy, wondering if the other kids had already paid the registration fee to Eddie. He couldn't see him anywhere.

"Your sponsor. You know, the business that wants to back you and donate money to our cause, just like the poster said. This year, the cause is the Kids' Hope Foundation."

"What?" said Billy.

"The Kids' Hope Foundation. The playground committee donates money to charity, and this year we've picked the Kids' Hope Foundation. That's an organization that grants wishes to kids who are sick. So they can have a dream come true."

"I don't have a sponsor," said Billy, his throat burning. "I guess . . . I guess I can't be in the contest."

"You don't have to have one for today," said Samantha, kindly. "Just get one signed up for Thursday, before the contest begins. Here, take one of our pamphlets. It explains everything."

Billy looked at the fine print. He picked out the word *and* a couple of times, but that was all. He stuffed the pamphlet into his pocket and headed for home.

"Good luck," called Samantha after him.

"Yeah," he muttered, without turning around. "Yeah. I'll need it." He went home slowly and sat numbly on the mat, carefully pulling on his socks and shoes, making sure to get the runners on the right feet. Then he walked all the way to Main Street and went up and down, looking into store windows, wondering who might want to sponsor him.

At the sporting goods shop, a man came out and asked if he needed help, but Billy could tell he really meant, "Stop hanging around here." Billy went into the golf shop and was chased out by a woman who said, "We're closed for carpet cleaning. Can't you read the sign?"

No, I can't read the sign, thought Billy miserably. I can't read anything. If I could read, I'd have known about the sponsor and I wouldn't be running out of time!

A dog was tied up in front of the post office. When Billy came close, it growled.

"Shut up," he told it, and the dog went crazy, barking and pulling on its chain.

"Quit teasing my dog!" a man said, coming out of the post office. "He bites kids like you."

Billy just shook his head and walked past, his insides a swirling tornado. Nobody on Main Street would be his sponsor, not in a million years.

Chapter Six

When Billy got home, his mouth tasted like sand and his feet were burning. His ankles hurt, too; he'd been holding his feet stiff, trying to keep the oversized runners from falling off. He went to his room and flopped down on the bed, but his legs wouldn't stay still. He got up and jumped around for a minute and then tried to lie down again, but it wouldn't work. There was nothing worse than being tired and having a body that kept on going.

"Billy, is that you?" called his mother from the shower. "I'm just getting cleaned up. I'll be out in a minute."

Billy went into the living room and leaped onto the back of the couch. From there, he somersaulted down onto the cushions, and then did it again.

"Billy Ray, what do you think you're doing!" said his mother, coming into the room. She rubbed at her wet hair with a towel. "Get off that couch right now. You're gonna break its back." As Billy flopped over in another somersault, she raised her voice. "I said, now!"

He collapsed on the floor at her feet, and pulled himself up into a handstand.

"Have you had some lunch?" she said, speaking to his toes as if they were a microphone. "I hope so, because if you haven't, we'll have to get out the oatmeal!"

Billy managed a small smile.

"I had Dutch pancakes at Mrs. Schmidt's," he said. "I helped her finish them off."

"No, you didn't," said his mother. "She was out all day, taking her husband for his checkup. I talked to her on my way in."

"Oh, yeah," said Billy. "I guess I meant the other day. I had pancakes there the other day."

"Come and eat something," said his mom. "You gotta put fuel in the tank, remember? Or your body can't run."

Yeah, right! thought Billy. I could be dead and I bet my legs would still be running.

His mother made him a ham sandwich and watched him eat it. Then she said, "Hey, I need you to run to the store and pick up some milk. We're all out." She got her purse and took out the wallet.

"Aw, please, no running," said Billy.

"I was sure I had a five dollar bill in here," his mother said, examining the rest of the purse. "I got it as change yesterday when I bought our lottery ticket. Billy? Do you know anything about this?"

Billy remembered what had happened to the money but he dropped down on all fours and shook his head.

"Are you sure?" his mother asked. "You didn't take the five dollars out of here?"

He shook his head again. Then he jumped back to his

feet and got up on the couch for another somersault.

"Billy Ray, you stop that right now! I bet you forgot to take your pill this morning."

"Aw, why do I need to take pills all the time," he complained. "Am I sick?"

When she didn't answer, he asked again, "Mom, am I sick?" And then he had an idea. "Because if I'm sick, there's this place that will help me find where Dad is."

"What?" his mother said sharply.

"There's this place. It's called the Kids' Hope Foundation. Samantha Peeteetuce told me about it. Sick kids can get wishes to come true, so that families can have fun."

His mother sighed.

"No, Billy, you're not sick." Now her voice had a heavy sound.

"But I gotta take pills!"

"Never mind. They're just to calm you down. There's nothing wrong with you!"

How come Mom's so grumpy all the time? Billy wondered. She never used to be so grumpy.

He scooted down onto the floor and crawled on his belly to the kitchen where his mother handed him the pill and a glass of water.

"Want a doughnut?" she asked, opening the box.

"Okay. How about three?" he said.

"Nope. One is plenty. Come on, sit up at the table with me and we'll each have one."

She watched him for a few minutes while he ate, but no matter how hard he tried he couldn't stay on his chair.

Soon he was under the table, and when his mother had finished her doughnut, she crawled under there with him.

"Oh, this is hard to do with my big belly," she said. "Come over here and I'll scratch your back."

"Okay," Billy said, sliding closer and sniffing at the smell of the soap his mother used on the floor. He liked it when she scratched his back, with lots of rubbing around the shoulder blades. She gave him a good workout and then she tickled him, and they both laughed. Then she stopped and gently tugged at his earlobe.

"Billy, listen. I don't think your dad is coming back," she said in a low voice. "I think maybe this time he's gone for good."

"Maybe he'll come back tomorrow," Billy said.

"No, I don't think so," she said.

Billy thought about the guitar sitting in the corner of the living room and his throat ached, as if he had swallowed a bunch of pebbles. Dad would be back. Billy just knew it. Unless something was wrong. Unless he was hurt or something. The idea that Dad could be hurt came to him sharp and dangerous, and it seemed as if one of those fault lines from the bedroom ceiling was opening up inside his head. He felt dizzy. Dad'll be back Thursday, for sure, he told himself. He'll be back on Thursday!

"I think he'll be back on Thursday," Billy muttered, but his mother didn't seem to hear him. She scratched his back a little more, but it didn't feel as good, and then she heaved herself out from under the table.

"If I don't get up now, I'll never get up," she said, gasping a little and rubbing her belly as she got to her feet.

Billy stayed under the table. He didn't want to talk anymore. He reached into his pocket and felt around until he held a penny between his fingers. He just wanted to be left alone. And he wanted his dad. More than anything, he wished Dad would come home.

Chapter Seven

When his mother went to lie down for a rest, Billy went to his room to practice his tricks. He was doing pretty well. He knew fifteen for sure, and the other six were coming along. All except *The CN Tower*, which was the hardest. The trick book showed pictures of how it was supposed to look. Sometimes he could match them, but sometimes he couldn't and his tower looked more like an igloo.

Suddenly he heard the apartment door open. Heavy steps entered, and a voice called out, "Chris—are you home?"

"Dad!" said Billy, jumping off his bed, but he stopped in the doorway. There was something in his father's tone that made him uncertain. He heard his mother's footsteps.

"You're back," he heard her say and the words hung coldly in the air, and then Dad said something that Billy couldn't make out over music from the radio, and then the sounds of an argument filled the apartment, like the cawing of crows.

"But I just need a little money!" Dad's voice was loud and clear now. "I just need a few bucks."

"I don't get paid for a couple of weeks!" Mom said. "And I need the money for the baby!"

"You should lighten up!" said Dad. "Let's have a few beers and celebrate."

"I'm not drinking, Zak, remember?" Billy could tell she was mad. Her voice had that silvery, sharp sound.

He remembered lots of times at night when Mom's voice had been as smooth as Dad's, and the sound of bottles and glasses from the kitchen would rattle around in his head like ice cubes until eventually there would be yelling, and sometimes laughter, and then, finally, he would sleep.

"Oh, come on, a few drinks won't hurt." Dad had gotten louder. He sounded drunk.

"No, I'm not kidding, Zak. Drinks would hurt the baby, and I'm gonna do the right thing."

Billy heard something crash and it sounded like Dad had broken something. A cup, maybe.

"Come on, let's have a little party!" he said. "This baby won't be like Billy, don't worry. Come on, lighten up!"

What did Dad mean by that? Billy leaned out into the hallway, trying to hear better.

"Zak, did you come in here earlier? Did you take some money out of my purse?" Mom asked.

"I'd never touch a lady's purse," Dad slurred.

"I'll bet you did. I'll bet you did take that money!" said Mom.

Billy heard a big crash and then Mom yelled, "You get out of here right now, you thief! Take your stuff and go, and don't come back!"

The doorbell rang. Before anyone could answer it, the door opened and Billy heard Mrs. Schmidt's voice.

"Chris, everything okay? I heard some loud noises."

"It's okay, Gladys." Billy could hardly hear Mom's voice over the sound of his own beating heart. "Everything is fine," he thought she said.

"Because I have some nice cookies just finishing and I was thinking you all should come on over and have some. There's too many for Pork Chop to eat, with him not feeling so good, and they're better when they're fresh."

"Zak was just leaving," said his mother, "but Billy and I would love to come."

Billy went out into the hall and saw his father leaning against the kitchen counter near an overturned chair. Billy took a step towards him, trying to think of what to say, but no words came.

"Take your stuff because I'm getting the locks changed," called Billy's mother. She grabbed Billy by the wrist and pulled him towards the door. His stomach hurt. Instead of looking at his dad, he looked in the corner of the living room at the guitar. It looked as it always did—caramel wood gleaming, the silver panel reflecting the light.

As they went out the door, Billy looked down at his feet. His mom was pulling him fast and the cut on his toe was bleeding again. He started to complain, but his mother pulled him hard, steering him into the Schmidts' apartment. Then Mrs. Schmidt closed the door behind them.

In the Schmidts' kitchen, Billy didn't see any cookies. In

the other room, Pork Chop was dozing in his easy chair in front of the television, dressed as always in a bow tie, white shirt, and creased black pants.

"You sit down and have a cup of tea," said Mrs. Schmidt.

"What kind of cookies are they?" asked Billy, even though he didn't want to eat anything right now. His stomach felt all swirly.

"Well, I guess all I have is these ones in the box," said Mrs. Schmidt, offering him a store-bought vanilla wafer.

"Billy, you have one and then we'll go for a walk or something," said his mother.

"You'll do no such thing," said Mrs. Schmidt. "You just sit down and have a cup of tea, and in a little while I'll get Pork Chop to go over there and make sure he's gone." Billy tried to say something but his voice had disappeared.

"Thank you, Gladys," said his mother, wearily, sitting down at the kitchen table. "Zak wasn't always like this. It's just the booze talking—at least that's what they say in my AA meetings."

Mrs. Schmidt nodded and patted her hand.

"You're a good friend," Chris went on. "How is your husband today?"

"Cancer's an unpredictable thing," said Mrs. Schmidt. "Sometimes he seems a little better, sometimes a little worse."

Billy went out and stood in the living room where he could see the TV. *Wheel of Fortune* was on. He tried to think about the prizes but he couldn't keep his mind on the show. The words Dad had said echoed in his head. *Don't worry, this baby won't turn out like Billy.* He tasted salt on his lips and blinked as more tears fell. Was Dad ashamed of him? *This baby won't turn out like Billy.*

But what if he won that contest? Then wouldn't Dad be proud of him? He was sure he could win. Then Dad would come back. Except that Mom thought Dad had stolen the money. She had kicked him out this time because she thought he'd stolen the money from her purse. Billy was glad Pork Chop was sleeping now and couldn't see him rubbing away the tears. Dad isn't coming back, he thought, and it's all my fault.

Chapter Eight

Later that night when they'd gone back to their apartment, more pennies from Mrs. Schmidt in his pocket, Billy was too restless to sleep. His secret from Mom, the reason why Dad wasn't coming back, sat heavily on his chest, making him feel as though he couldn't breathe.

He waited until his mother had gone to bed and then he went outside. At first he thought there wasn't a moon and he stood in the gray night and looked at the sky. The air seemed to be vibrating around him, like a giant moth, and he shivered in his thin T-shirt. The sky was full of small clouds—a mackerel sky, Mrs. Schmidt would call it, because the clouds looked like scales on a fish's back.

Then one of the clouds shifted and the moon swelled into view, bigger than the other night, a golden, lopsided oval. He stood on the sidewalk and stared at it and as he looked, he thought he could see a face on the moon. The face of a boy with slanted eyes. A face like his own.

The moon looked heavy, as if it was tilting out of the sky. As heavy as my secret, he thought, and sighed. Why did everything have to be so bad?

Billy pulled the yo-yo out of his pocket and started to do some tricks.

"I'll show them," he said. "I'll show everyone." He started to sing that suede shoes song his dad liked, and as he sang, he felt the power flow into his arms and hands. As if the yo-yo had a life of its own, it performed each trick perfectly. Twenty-one tricks.

"It's BILLY RAY, THE AMAZING YO-YO MASTER," Billy said. "Here to show you his twenty-one amazing tricks."

Billy heard a noise behind him. He whirled around and there, like a ghost emerging from the darkness, was Natasha, standing on the other side of the street.

"You scared me," he called. "I thought you were a murderer or something."

At first, Billy thought the sound he heard was a meadowlark, but then he realized it couldn't be a meadowlark, not at night. It was Natasha, laughing.

"What's so funny?" he asked, crossing the street. "What are you laughing at?" In the moonlight her eyelashes made soft shadows on her cheeks.

She stopped laughing and gazed at him with her glistening eyes. Then she looked up at the sky.

"The moon has gotten big, eh?" he said. "I was looking at it too. I was thinking it kind of looks like me. The face on it, I mean."

Natasha shook her head, and pointed to herself.

"You think it looks like you? Come on, it does not," Billy said, looking at her large, round eyes, her small heart-shaped face, her hair smooth as the feathers of a bird's wing.

Natasha shook her head again and cupped one hand behind her ear.

"You think it sounds like you? Yeah, well you might be right about that. You're as quiet as the moon, that's for sure."

He heard the meadowlark sound again, and watched as she laughed. She looked nice, laughing. Being happy suited her.

He wished he felt like laughing, but he didn't. He cleared his throat, but there wasn't a laugh anywhere in there. The weight from the secret he was keeping from his mother was still heavy on his chest, and it made him feel hot inside. He swallowed and took a deep breath.

"I got something to be sad about," he said. "It didn't start out to be a secret, but it is, now. I took money from Mom's purse, and she thought Dad stole it, and now she's kicked him out. I don't know what I'm gonna do."

Natasha looked at him and shook her head.

"Do you think I should say?" he asked. "Say to Mom that I did it?"

Natasha stood still and he could tell that she was thinking hard. Then she nodded her head.

"But I'll get into trouble," Billy said. "She'll be real mad."

Natasha shrugged.

"So you think it won't matter that my mom gets mad? You don't know my mom. She can get real mad."

Natasha turned, as if to go back to her house.

"Wait! I'll think about it, okay?" Billy said. "I'll think about it."

Natasha reached out and put her hand on Billy's arm. It rested there for just for a moment, and her touch felt soft and cool.

"I'll see you tomorrow, okay?" he said as she took a step away. "Tomorrow, you'll be here?"

Natasha nodded. A car sped by, its taillights two red eyes blinking in the darkness. Billy turned and crossed the street behind it, taking slow, careful steps. A cloud passed across the moon, and when he looked back to see if Natasha was still there, she had disappeared.

• • •

The next morning, Billy crawled into bed with his mother and he could hardly get the words out.

"I did it," he said, finally.

"What, honey?" said his mom, sleepily. "Did you have a bad dream?"

"No, I took that money. I took it from your purse." Billy took a deep breath. "Because it was for the registration fee and I had to enter. I had to enter the contest so Dad would come back, and now he's gone because I took the money!"

His mother sat up and pulled on her robe.

"That's not good," she said, finally. "You know that taking something from someone else is stealing!"

"But now Dad can come home, right?" Billy asked. "You're not mad at him anymore?"

His mother stood and went to the window. Then she came and sat beside him on the bed.

"It's not so simple," she said. "Billy, your dad has some problems he's going to have to figure out before he comes back to us. One of them is his drinking. I know how it is. I used to drink like that, too, but I'm on the wagon and it's better for all of us. Better for the baby, for sure." She patted her stomach.

Dad's words came flooding back. "Did he leave because he hates me?" Billy asked in a small voice. "Because I'm so stupid?"

"Of course not!" Mom exclaimed, turning to face him. "And you're not stupid."

"I am stupid!" Billy yelled. "I can't even read the pamphlet about the contest, that's how stupid I am! I can't read the words on a Cheez Whiz jar, or the words in a shop window, and I can't even write my own address!"

"Billy, I know you have trouble with some things. But you're not stupid!" Her eyes filled with tears and she turned away.

"I am so stupid!" he screamed. "Do you know what it's like? There's stuff everywhere that people are reading and I can't figure it out. And people are always mad at me!"

"It's not your fault," his mother whispered. "Oh, Billy, listen. It's not your fault."

"Well, whose fault is it?" cried Billy. "If it's not my fault, whose fault is it that I put my shoes on the wrong feet and that I can't sit still. Whose fault is it that the only words I can read are baby words?"

"Billy," said his mother, and stopped. Then she took a deep breath and went on. "I guess . . . I guess it's my fault," she said, and a tear rolled down her cheek. "We . . . we didn't know better, but I guess it's time to tell you. When I was pregnant with you, I did a lot of drinking. Maybe it affected you, I'm not sure, but the doctors . . . they said . . . they said it did." A sob broke from his mother's throat, and Billy stared at her, numb.

"Is that . . . is that what happened to my heart?" Billy asked in a whisper.

"Maybe." His mother brushed a sleeve over her eyes. "We don't know. Booze is so bad for babies. But your heart's okay, now. Your heart is better than most people's. You don't have to worry about that."

"I wish I was somebody else," Billy said, and he would have said more but he could feel his voice dwindling away until there was nothing left.

"You are who you are," his mother said. "And you can do lots of things real well. You can be who you want to be, as long as you put your mind to it."

Billy rolled away from her and off the bed. He ran out to the living room because there was nowhere else to run, and threw himself down on the couch. The rough fabric scratched his forehead.

After a little while, his mother leaned over him and hugged him, and he felt her wet cheeks soak through his shirt. "We're a team, Billy, you and me. And we'll be okay. I've got a good job, and later, after I have the baby, I'm gonna go back to school. No matter what, we'll be okay."

"Why are you going back to school?" he blurted. "You're smart, Mom."

"Getting smarter all the time," she said. "Come on, let's get some breakfast. I'm hungry for a grilled Cheez Whiz sandwich. You want one?" He shook his head, but he rolled off the couch and followed her into the kitchen.

As Billy stood at the counter and ate toast and jam, he thought about what she'd said. He didn't want to think about all of it. He tried not to think about Dad not coming home. Or the part about how Mom had been drinking when she was pregnant with him. Instead he thought of something Mrs. Schmidt said: "All God's creatures have a place in the choir."

Maybe I do, thought Billy. And maybe I don't. What good am I anyways, if I can't read and if I do stupid things all the time?

Unless I win that contest. Then I'll have twenty-five bucks. That'd show 'em. That'd show 'em all!

Suddenly he remembered the pamphlet and pulled it out of his pocket, along with the new pennies Mrs. Schmidt had given him. He thought about what he should wish for and closed his eyes.

When his mother came back into the kitchen, dressed for work, he held the pamphlet out to her.

"There's lots of 'ands' in it," he said.

"Uh-huh. Here, let's see," she said. She read aloud about the sponsorship program, and how businesses were encouraged to pledge money to the North Battleford Community Playground to be donated to the Kids' Hope Foundation when the contest was over. There was a space at the back for a business to fill out its name and enter the amount of money it was pledging.

"This sounds okay," said his mother. "So the contest is Thursday at four o'clock. Too bad I'll be working or I'd come and watch. But it doesn't say anything here about a registration fee. How much did you say you spent? Five dollars?"

"Yeah," said Billy.

"Well you'll have to pay me back somehow," she said. "And what business are you gonna ask to sponsor you?"

"I don't know," said Billy. "I have to think about it."

"Uh-huh," said his mother. "It says this has to be completed by Thursday, before the contest. Or you can't participate."

"Maybe I'm not going to enter the contest after all," said Billy. "Not if I have to go by myself."

His mother looked at him sadly.

"If you want to win that contest, you should go and try." She sighed. "Look, I'm gonna go to work now, but when I get home we could try and think of who your sponsor could be."

"It's already Tuesday," Billy said. "I need to find someone now, if I'm going to enter."

"I promise I'll help you later," said his mom, "but I just don't have time right now. Hey, it's gonna be hot again today. Why don't you come swim at the hotel?" Billy shook his head. He didn't want to swim in that crummy pool and he didn't want to talk to his mother anymore. What she'd said to him before, about why he was different, came back like big gray clouds blocking out the sun: *Booze is bad for babies.*

"I don't want you to be alone all day," she said. "You're alone too much now your dad's gone."

"I'm okay," he said, balling up the last of his toast and dropping it into the garbage.

"Well, then, later on you should go visit Mrs. Schmidt," she said. "Promise?"

Billy nodded and his mother took her key off the hook. She looked as if she were going to say something else, but she squeezed her lips together and went out the door without saying anything at all. As Billy stood staring at the closed door, the clouds around his thoughts suddenly parted and he could think clearly again. He carefully wound the string around his yo-yo as if he were wrapping a present, and then walked into the living room.

As long as I put my mind to it, he said to himself and clenched his teeth. On Thursday, I'm going to win that contest, and Dad will be there. He promised. I know he'll be there.

Billy's voice, when he started to sing, cracked like a branch on a windy day. After a while, though, he forgot about his father and just sang. And for a little while, he felt good again. Lighter, now that he wasn't carrying that heavy secret about taking the money. Then he looked into the corner of the room and his voice broke. His dad's guitar was gone.

Chapter Nine

Natasha was already out on her front steps when Billy went outside. She was sucking honey from the small yellow caragana flowers from the hedge. There weren't many of them left. Soon there would be pods in their place, with seeds inside. Billy used to watch the pods split when they'd had a hedge like that behind the apartment building. He'd tried sucking on those flowers before, too, but it took so long to get any taste that he soon gave up.

"Natasha," he called. "Is your dad home?"

Natasha shook her head.

"He's gone? He goes to work this early on Tuesdays?" Billy asked.

Natasha nodded, spitting a yellow bud into the grass.

"Well, I've gotta talk to him! Can you take me there? To his car business?"

Natasha looked at him with a surprised expression. Then she nodded.

"Okay, right now?" said Billy.

Natasha turned and glanced in the direction of her house, but Mrs. Arnold wasn't anywhere in sight. Waving him after her, the girl headed off down the street, and Billy followed.

The sun glanced off the pavement and made the air look as if it were melting. Billy squinted his eyes and pretended he was in the desert, on an expedition.

"If you were in the desert and you could only have one thing with you, what would it be?" asked Billy. When Natasha didn't answer, he went on.

"I think the top three things would be water, a knife, and a car. Which would you pick, if you could only have one?"

Natasha looked at him and shrugged.

"I'd pick the knife, because you could protect yourself," said Billy. They passed another hedge of yellow flowers and Natasha stopped to pick a few, but Billy motioned her onwards.

"We've gotta hurry," he said.

As they walked, he told Natasha all about the contest and how he was going to win as long as he could get a sponsor. After that, he hummed the tune his dad usually played for him, and then sang. It was an old Elvis song, and it had been his dad's favorite.

> *Well it's a one for the money,*
> *Two for the show,*
> *Three to get ready, now,*
> *Go cat go,*
> *But doncha*
> *Step on my blue suede shoes.*

He remembered Dad singing it at home when they practiced Billy's tricks. He remembered so clearly that he thought Dad might be with him now, playing just the way he used to and singing along. The song felt calm and sure in his throat, and for just a minute it felt like it was sung by two voices. Two voices in one. Power surged through his body as he pulled the Typhoon out of his pocket. He was good at these tricks! He could do them all!

"Is everybody ready for the amazing Billy Ray, Yo-yo Master?" Billy said in a deep voice, Dad's voice. "He's here to perform for you his twenty-one amazing tricks!"

Natasha put her hands together and clapped, and Billy wound the string. As they walked along, he tried one trick after another, running ahead now and then and letting Natasha catch up. He could do all twenty-one of them! He really was an amazing yo-yo master!

> *You can do anything*
> *But stay off my blue suede shoes!*

He stopped singing when they reached the car dealership. It took up a whole block and he sucked in his breath at the sight of all those new cars, gleaming in the sun.

"Wow!" he exclaimed. "That's really something!" He had never walked this far from home before, and he wondered if he could ever find this place again by himself. How he'd love to spend time walking up and down, smelling the new car smells and comparing colors. Bright red, orange-red, cherry-red, rust. He'd never before seen so many variations on one color.

Natasha led him up to the main doors and they pulled them open and walked inside. The floor gleamed with polish and Billy breathed deeply, thinking how much the showroom smelled like Dad's shaving kit.

"Wow!" he said, again.

One of the salesmen, a man in a brown suit, came walking over.

"Can I help you kids with anything?" he asked. Then he recognized Natasha.

"Hey, your dad's in his office. You and your friend can go right in."

Natasha walked down a hall to an office with a big green door. Billy followed. She opened the door and they saw Mr. Arnold sitting at a huge wooden desk that was covered with papers. He looked startled to see them.

"Natasha? What's this all about?" he asked. "What are you doing here?"

Natasha looked at Billy, and then went and got herself a drink at the water cooler in the corner of the room.

"It was . . . I asked her to bring me here," Billy stammered. "I have to talk to you about something. It's business," he said.

Mr. Arnold looked surprised.

"Business, eh?" he said. "Are you in the market for a new car, son? Go ahead, sit down." When he smiled, his very red cheeks looked like crab apples.

Billy shook his head.

"No, I'd better stand. So this is the thing. I have this pamphlet here—" he took the pamphlet from his pocket and put it on top of some of the papers on the desk between them. "I have this pamphlet that tells all about it. But what I want is for your business to sponsor me in a talent contest. It's at the park, and I'm going to do yo-yo tricks. And I think I can win."

"Uh-huh," said Mr. Arnold. "And what's this sponsorship all about?"

"It says right there," said Billy. "The money goes to the Kids' Hope Foundation, where they give wishes to sick kids. Without a sponsor, I can't enter the contest. And I want to enter. My dad's coming."

"I see," said Mr. Arnold, looking at the pamphlet. "Well, I'll have to give it some thought. How much money would you be wanting?"

"I think a whole lot," said Billy. "But it depends on you. They don't actually say."

"I see," said Mr. Arnold again. "Well, as I said, I'll give it some thought. But in the meantime, we'd better get my daughter home. I'll call her mother and let her know she's on her way. I don't expect you two asked her permission to come down here."

Billy shook his head. He hadn't even thought about whether Natasha should ask permission. He looked over at her. She had finished the water and as he watched, she threw the cup into the garbage can across the room. A perfect ringer!

"Ten points!" said Billy. She flashed him a smile.

When Mr. Arnold hung up the phone, he turned to Natasha.

"Your mother's not very happy," he said. "She's been looking all over for you, and you've got a doctor's appointment in half an hour. We'd better hurry."

"Another doctor's appointment," said Billy. "You must be really sick!"

Natasha kicked at the carpet, and waited for her father to lock his filing cabinet. Then they followed him out to the car. Billy stared at Mr. Arnold's neck where it bulged over the back of his tight collar. He wondered if it hurt.

Billy had never before been in such a fancy car. On the outside it was shiny and gray, and on the inside the dashboard had all sorts of buttons and levers that Billy ached to touch. Instead of trying to touch them, though, he sat on his hands and kept quiet, breathing in the rich, leathery smell.

"Where should I drop you off?" Mr. Arnold asked. "You live right across the street from us, don't you?"

"What's wrong with Natasha?" Billy blurted, his arms and legs aching from trying to keep still. "I mean, how come she's gotta go to the doctor so many times?"

"It's kind of private, son," said Mr. Arnold. "She's not really sick in the way you might be thinking. That is, she doesn't have anything catching."

"Oh, that's good," said Billy. "Because I sure wouldn't want to catch something before the contest."

"Now, let's see," said Mr. Arnold. "Your name is . . ."

"Billy Ray," said Billy. "But my first name is really—" for a moment he couldn't remember, but then, like a basketball dropping through a hoop, it came to him. "William," he said.

"Okay, William Ray, here's our stop."

Mr. Arnold parked the car in front of their house and Billy got out. Mrs. Arnold came running down the driveway and Billy thought she looked mad.

"She's right here safe and sound, Mother," Mr. Arnold said, opening the car door. Billy glanced both ways for traffic and then darted across the street as if something was chasing him. When he'd climbed the steps of his apartment building, he turned to wave at Natasha, but the Arnolds' car had already pulled away.

Chapter Ten

That afternoon, Billy watched for the big gray car to come home. Lots of cars passed his window, but never a gray one. At two o'clock when the Arnolds' car still hadn't pulled into the driveway, he finally gave up and tapped on the Schmidts' door.

"My mom said I should come visit," he said when Mrs. Schmidt's familiar shape filled the doorway. "What are you doing today?"

"Well, I've just finished the ironing and now I'm thinking about baking some cookies," she said, giving him her wide smile. "Isn't that a coincidence! Come on in and see what I got by special delivery this morning."

Billy followed her into the living room where Pork Chop was dozing in front of the TV. Today he was wearing a red velvet bow tie with his crisp white shirt. Six other white shirts were hanging on metal hangers from the curtain rod, and Mrs. Schmidt folded up the ironing board and propped it against the wall.

"Look at these," she said, lifting the cover on the couch. Instead of regular feet, the couch had little pink pigs' hooves.

"They're funny!" laughed Billy. "Where'd you get 'em?"

"My daughter's husband," said Mrs. Schmidt. "They sent them in the mail for my birthday."

"Is today your birthday?" asked Billy.

Mrs. Schmidt nodded.

"Happy Birthday!" said Billy. He thought of the words to the birthday song that ended with: *You look like a monkey, and you smell like one, too*, and he dug his fingernails into his palms so he wouldn't blurt them out. He knew Mrs. Schmidt wouldn't think they were funny. It was a losing battle, though, but just as he began: *You look like a monkey* . . . the phone rang. While he turned away, the words bubbling up in his throat, Mrs. Schmidt picked up the receiver, said a few words, smiled, and then hung up.

"My daughter, Daisy," she said. "Just calling to make sure I'm having a good day."

Mrs. Schmidt's kitchen always smelled of lemons and today was no exception. Billy followed her to the table where he sat on one of the wicker kitchen chairs and studied the pigs. There were pottery pigs on the counter, holding coffee and tea. There were pig fridge magnets on the fridge, holding up lists. There was even a set of pig curtains over the window that opened towards the parking lot.

After he studied the pigs, Billy looked at Mrs. Schmidt's hair. It was curly, and each curl lay on her head in a perfect ringlet.

"Your hair looks like snails," he said.

"Snails aren't gray," was her reply, "but if the Good Lord wanted me to have brown hair until I died, he'd have made it so. My dear sister, may she rest in peace, didn't have a strand of gray until she was sixty. She was the lucky one."

"I like gray," said Billy. "It looks soft. And it's a good color for cars."

"Well, thank you, honey," said Mrs. Schmidt. "You have a silver tongue."

Billy stuck out his tongue to see if it was silver. It wasn't—at least what he could see of it wasn't. Just pink, as usual.

"Now do you want peanut butter or chocolate chip?" she asked.

He thought for a minute. Peanut butter cookies crumbled and melted in your mouth. With the chocolate chips, though, you could eat away the cookie parts and then suck on the chips at the end.

"Could you put chocolate chips in the peanut butter ones?" he asked.

"Well, bless my soul, I suppose I could. Now that's a real good idea," said Mrs. Schmidt. "I think Pork Chop would like that combination."

She got out her big white mixing bowl and a wooden spoon with a pig's head for a handle. He watched for a few minutes as she measured ingredients and then his legs wouldn't let him sit any longer.

"Is Mr. Schmidt still watching TV?" he asked, going over to the hall.

"I think he's gone into the bedroom," said Mrs. Schmidt.

"Being sick is hard on him. Sometimes he just needs to lie down."

"He's got cancer, right?" asked Billy, after a while.

"That's right. He's a fighter, though."

"When you have cancer, it's not catching, is it?" asked Billy.

"No, cancer's not catching. You got nothing to worry about."

Billy thought for a minute before he spoke.

"I think that Natasha might have cancer," he said, finally. "She's the girl across the street. The one you said was from Romania, from the orphanage. She's always going to the doctor."

"Well, you know those children from the orphanages can have lots of troubles. I heard about it on TV," said Mrs. Schmidt. "This program I watched said the kids were never given enough to eat, and when they come to Canada many of them have a hard time eating. Doesn't make sense, does it? You'd think that people who were starved would eat too much when they got a chance, wouldn't you? Poor motherless kids."

"Natasha's got a mother. Over there in Romania," said Billy.

"Oh," said Mrs. Schmidt. "Well, now, I guess that could be true," she went on. "Lots of those children weren't really orphans. The TV show said that many of them had parents who were too poor to look after them, bless their little hearts."

"Natasha's mother left her in a box at a church," said Billy, "when she was just a baby."

"My goodness," said Mrs. Schmidt. "Natasha must sure like you to tell you all of that."

"I think it was a secret," said Billy. "But it just got too heavy for her so she told me. You won't tell, will you?"

"My lips are sealed," said Mrs. Schmidt, and smiled.

"Where is Romania?" asked Billy as he used a fork to flatten the cookies Mrs. Schmidt had put on the pan.

"Well, now, I'm not too sure," she said. "I guess it's over there on the other side of the world." She picked up a rag and wiped the counter.

"It's a long way, then," said Billy. He thought for a minute. "I guess Natasha must have left her voice over there. She can make sounds, but she doesn't talk at all."

"Is that so?" said Mrs. Schmidt. "Well, I heard that voices can come and go, depending on how you're feeling. Maybe she has memories that make her sad."

Billy thought about that. He wondered if Natasha's memories were all sad. Then he remembered that she thought a lot about her mother. Those memories wouldn't be so sad! But maybe the best memories made you the saddest! Like when he thought about how his dad used to take him to the circus, and swimming—and the fried mushrooms they'd make in the kitchen with the radio on full blast.

"Well, she's looked after now, anyways," said Mrs. Schmidt. "They have more money than you could shake a stick at."

Billy wondered why anybody would want to shake a stick at money, but he kept quiet. Mrs. Schmidt might say funny things sometimes, but she made the best cookies he'd ever had.

The chocolate chip peanut butter cookies were no exception. "Right on!" he mumbled as he took his first bite. After he'd had six of them, he remembered about watching for the Arnolds' car to come home and he told Mrs. Schmidt he had to go.

"Come back anytime," she said. "Later today, if you like. We'll be here, Pork Chop and me. And stay out of trouble, honey. Never look a pigpen in the eye."

Billy thought about that as he opened the door to his apartment. How could you look a pigpen in the eye? Well, maybe by crawling around in the muck, that was how. And he sure wasn't going to be doing any of that! He went straight to his living room window, but the driveway across the street was still empty.

Must be a long doctor's appointment, he said to himself. *Or maybe they've gone out for ice cream.* He hoped Natasha wasn't too sick to eat ice cream.

The apartment was too quiet, and he went to the kitchen and turned on the radio. Dad always kept the radio on when he was home. Billy missed the music. He missed his dad. He wished he'd said something to his dad when he was here yesterday. He'd wanted to say something, but he couldn't find his voice. And now it was too late. Dad was gone and there was no way to even say good-bye.

With a bumpy feeling in his stomach, Billy went outside and hung around by the front steps for a while, where the feeling twisted into anger. Why didn't they come home?

He had to talk to Mr. Arnold and it just couldn't wait! He walked up and down the sidewalk and it was so hot that sweat trickled down inside his shirt. He did a somersault, but the dry grass prickled his hands.

It was supposed to be cool in the desert at night, and Billy thought about that for a while. What would it really be like? Of the three things he could take with him—water, a knife, or a car—he'd pick the car. A good car, with tires that would run on sand. He wouldn't need a knife, or water, as much as he'd need the car. And it wouldn't have to be a new car, either. Just a plain old car that could get him safely out of there.

Chapter Eleven

It was dark when the Arnolds' car pulled into their driveway. Billy had gone back to the window for the hundredth time when he saw it arrive. Mom was in the bathroom soaking her feet in cool water. Her ankles looked puffy.

"It's just from the heat," she said. "And being pregnant. My feet don't hurt but I need to soak them so they don't swell even more."

"I'm going outside for a minute," said Billy. "Across the street to see my friend. I'll be right back."

"Well, don't be long," she called. "It's nearly bedtime."

Billy ran up Natasha's steps and rang the doorbell. Mrs. Arnold answered the door, her thin, pale face unsmiling.

"Is Natasha's father in?" Billy asked.

"Why, yes," said Mrs. Arnold. "But it's a bit late. Can it wait until tomorrow?"

"No," said Billy. "No, please, I need to speak to him now."

"Well, for just a moment, but you should be on your way home soon. It's going to storm," she said. Then she stepped back into the house.

"Gerry!" she called, in a low voice. "That boy is here to see you."

She led Billy down the hall and into a living room that made him stop and look around in awe. Everything was gleaming wood: the floor, the furniture, the mantel over a rich, black fireplace.

"Wow!" he breathed. "This is nice!"

"Thank you," said Mrs. Arnold, a bit stiffly. "Please sit down. My husband will be right with you."

"I can't sit down," said Billy. "I'm too hyper, but even though I take pills I'm not sick. Thanks for inviting me in."

Mrs. Arnold looked at him for a minute, and then stepped back into the hallway. "I don't know what's keeping him," she said. "I'll just go and call again."

In a minute, Mr. Arnold appeared in the doorway. He was breathing heavily, as if he'd just climbed a lot of stairs, and he looked surprised to see Billy.

"Well, son," he breathed. "Now, what's this all about?"

"I need to know if you'll be my sponsor," Billy said, just as breathlessly. "Tomorrow is Wednesday, and I have to have a sponsor by Thursday, in time for the contest."

"I'm not sure it's something our company wishes to endorse," said Mr. Arnold. "We have to be very careful about where we spend our money, because if we're not, we soon won't have any money left. And then we wouldn't have a business, now, would we?"

Billy didn't understand everything Mr. Arnold was saying, but he knew that a *No* was hidden in the words.

"Well, could I please have my pamphlet back, then?" he asked in a voice that shook as if a wind were blowing it away. "Because it's the only one I have and I'll need it for finding another sponsor."

"Well, I left it at work, son," said Mr. Arnold. "I'll try and remember to bring it home tomorrow."

"Please remember it," said Billy, looking at him with desperate eyes. "I really need it by tomorrow."

When he got back to the apartment, his mother was sitting on the couch, her legs up on a chair.

"Your legs look like balloons, Mom," said Billy.

"Never mind. They'll get better soon." She sighed. "I hope."

"What if they don't?" asked Billy. "Will you have to quit your job?"

"I don't know," she said, wearily. "Never mind. You don't have to worry about it."

"I still need a sponsor," said Billy. "I don't know who to ask, but I have to find one by tomorrow. What'll I do?"

"Billy, I know I said I'd help you, but I'm just not feeling good," said his mother. "I don't know who you could get, but maybe tomorrow we'll think of somebody."

The lights flickered and then there was a crack of thunder.

"Go get the flashlight from under the sink," said his mom. "In case the power goes out."

"But you promised you'd help!" said Billy. "And I don't have a lot of time! If Dad were here he'd help."

"I'm just not able to help right now," said his mother

crossly. "I checked at work, but they're already sponsoring someone. Why don't you ask down at the store?" She leaned forward and began rubbing her legs.

"Yeah, maybe. I'll go there in the morning," said Billy, hopefully. "I bet they will. I bet they'll be my sponsor."

"Now go get that flashlight," said his mother as the lights shivered again.

Instead of going to bed, Billy opened his window and released the moths that had gathered on the glass. It wasn't raining yet, but you could smell it in the air, that slightly smoky smell that meant rain was coming. Billy looked across the street. There was no movement from Natasha's house. He stared so hard he thought his eyeballs were going to fall out.

Finally, as if feeling the power of his gaze, the curtains opened in an upstairs window. There was a light inside that made a silhouette out of the person standing there, and he knew it was her. He waved, but she didn't see him and just kept on standing there.

After a little while, the curtains opened in another upstairs window and Billy saw two more silhouettes. Mr. and Mrs. Arnold, standing there, looking up at the sky, too. Billy felt sadness come out of that house as if it were smoke, stinging his eyes. He watched the three of them until he could bear it no longer, and then he flung himself back on the bed.

What was Natasha thinking, looking up at the sky? Was she looking at the moon? He wondered if there was a full moon tonight, and if Natasha was going to draw a picture of it in her journal. Maybe she'd draw Raven, underneath the moon, holding it up, like in that story his teacher had told.

From his window, he could see storm clouds gathering like a great, dark herd of something. Right beside them, though, were clusters of stars. There were so many stars he couldn't count them all; they were like eyes that saw all of North Battleford, as well as the whole world—Romania, too, where Natasha had come from.

Maybe Natasha's mother was looking at the same sky and missing her daughter. Billy thought about the sadness of it all, and when he finally rolled over and went to sleep, he dreamed about a world so tiny that he could walk from one side to the other, where his father would be waiting for him.

Chapter Twelve

On Wednesday, Billy woke up sweating, his covers wrapped around him as tightly as if he were a caterpillar in a cocoon. He tore them off and stumbled out to the kitchen for a drink of water. His mother had already eaten and she was sitting at the table with her feet propped up on a chair.

"They're a little better," she said, "but I didn't sleep too good. I might not go to work today."

"You've gotta help me find a sponsor!" said Billy, staring at the dark circles under her eyes.

"Nope, I've just got to take it easy. Why don't you try the store, like I told you? I'll have to call in sick and then I'm going back to bed."

Billy swallowed his pill and ate a bowl of Shreddies. Then he threw on a pair of shorts and a T-shirt, and went outside. It had rained in the night. You could tell because the dirt in the gutters was packed down and still damp. The sun was out now, though, and it was going to be hot again.

Billy wished it would rain all day. He wished it would rain and rain, and he'd run out in it and feel the cool drops on his skin.

Billy kicked along the gutter to the store, stopping every now and then to check under the dirt for earthworms. When he found one, he carefully put it over on the grass in someone's yard. Better there than in the street, he figured, where cars could drive over them. On one lawn there was a robin, and he saved the worm for next door. His worms weren't gonna be anybody's breakfast.

He loved walking up and down the aisles in the store, loved how the food was all lined up on the shelves and how everything had its place. For a few minutes he forgot what he came for and just walked around, admiring the patterns things made. There were seven water guns hanging from hooks at the end of one of the aisles. He'd sure like to own one of those!

Suddenly Billy remembered the contest and why he'd come to the store in the first place. He checked the bulletin board where the poster had been but it was gone. Then he asked one of the cashiers if the store would like to sponsor him.

"You'll have to ask the manager," said the cashier, cracking her bubblegum. "Her desk is over there." She pointed, chewed for a few seconds, and then added, "And she should be back soon if you're lucky."

Billy went over to the counter and waited. There were some entry slips and a draw drum beside his elbow, and he figured he should enter his name and phone number. You never knew, he just might be a winner.

"B-i-l-l-y R-a-y," he printed. If he concentrated hard, he could get his phone number right, too.

"Can I help you?" said a gravelly voice. The manager stood before him, watching as he painfully formed his phone number.

"I . . . uh . . . I thought I'd enter your contest," stammered Billy.

"Well, good luck," she said, putting on her glasses.

"But that's not really why I'm here!" said Billy, quickly stuffing the paper into the draw drum. "I'm here because I need to ask if the store will give me some money. I mean, the money wouldn't really go to me, but I'd take it to the park."

The manager took off her glasses and looked at Billy. Billy knew he wasn't making much sense, and he tried harder, wishing he had the pamphlet with him.

"It's a talent contest," he said, trying to slow down. "And I have to have money to enter. At least, first I had to pay some money to enter, the five dollars that I got out of my mom's purse, but I need more money and I'm supposed to ask you for it."

"Sorry, can't help you," said the manager.

"But my mom said the store would be a good place to ask . . ." Billy started, putting his hand into his pocket to feel the comforting shape of the Typhoon.

"Sorry, we don't do that kind of thing," said the manager. She turned back to her desk and put on her glasses. Then she opened a filing cabinet and started looking through the files.

Billy walked out of the store without looking back. He tried to think of another place he could ask to sponsor him but he couldn't.

He found an old pop can on the street and kicked it as hard as he could. The noise was satisfying, a hollow ringing sound that made him feel like kicking it again, so he did.

He kicked the pop can all the way home and then pushed it down the drain of a storm sewer, but although he waited to hear it hit the bottom, the sound never came. Must have gotten stuck somewhere on the way down, he thought. Figures. I just can't do anything right.

He walked past Natasha's house without seeing her on the front steps, and it wasn't until he'd gone past and she ran behind and threw a pebble at him that he knew she was there.

"What's that for?" he asked.

She came up beside him and held out her notebook.

"I don't want to look at your old notebook right now. I don't have a sponsor and your dad has my pamphlet. Now I'm never gonna get a sponsor, and so I can't enter the contest!"

Natasha looked at him for a moment and then shook her head. She shook it again, more firmly, when Billy started walking again, but he ignored her. Then she threw another pebble at him but he kept walking.

"I'll help you," she said as he started to cross the street. He stopped in his tracks and swung around.

"What did you say?" he asked, surprised to hear her voice.

"I'll help you," she said, again. "Come on."

She turned and ran into the house, with Billy at her heels. Someone was playing the piano and Billy could hear the notes following one another, as if it were raining music.

When Natasha opened the door to the piano room, the music stopped.

"What is it?" asked Mrs. Arnold, looking at them around a big bouquet of pink roses that stood on the black, shiny surface of the piano. "Oh, you've brought your friend in? That's fine—you can get him some lemonade. But don't go away anywhere, because I won't know where you are."

Natasha shook her head.

"Yes, your friend can have one of the doughnuts we bought," said Mrs. Arnold. "But just one, okay? And tell him to keep that yo-yo in his pocket." Billy looked down, surprised to find himself winding the string of the Typhoon without knowing he was doing it.

"We don't want any chips on the furniture," Mrs. Arnold said. Then she started playing the piano again.

Natasha shook her head again, and then she narrowed her eyes and stamped her foot.

"No!" yelled Natasha. "No! Stop it. Stop!"

Mrs. Arnold stood up, bumping the sheet music and sending it flying onto the carpet.

"What? What did you . . . Natasha . . . you're talking! Oh, you're talking!" She ran around the piano and bent down, putting her arms around the girl's thin shoulders.

"Call Dad," Natasha said, her back stiff and straight. "Please call Dad." Her voice was softer than a moment ago, and musical, like birdsong.

"Oh, yes! I will! Just keep talking, darling. Please, keep talking. You have . . . you have such a lovely voice."

Mrs. Arnold got to her feet and hurried out to the kitchen. They could hear her on the phone to Natasha's dad.

"Gerry, she's talking again! After almost a year! She talked to me . . . she did . . . just now!"

Natasha led Billy to the kitchen and held open the bag of doughnuts. He picked a caramel one. When he bit into it, the icing cracked like an earthquake had struck. He licked at the sweet flakes that melted in his mouth, and then he bit into the doughnut and chewed.

Soon they heard the car pull up in the driveway and Mrs. Arnold ran and opened the front door.

"Hurry, Gerry. She's in the kitchen," she called. Mr. Arnold came into the kitchen, his crab apple cheeks even redder than before. He brushed past Billy and stood in front of Natasha.

"I'm home," he said. "Is your mother right? She's not . . . you're . . . you're talking again?"

"Please," said Natasha, and burst into tears.

"You'd better go, now," Mrs. Arnold said to Billy. "I think you'd better go. Thank you for . . . for coming over. We'll invite you back another day." She quickly moved him towards the back door. Before he knew it, Billy was in the yard, with the door to the house shut firmly behind him. He stood looking for a while at the windows, but none of the curtains moved.

As he walked around to the front of the house, he

wondered how a person could stop talking for almost a year. That was twelve months. A long time not to talk. As he passed the front of the house, he saw Natasha's notebook lying on the front steps where she must have dropped it. He went over and picked it up. *Wednesday July 19*, he read carefully. That was today. He couldn't read what Natasha had written underneath, but he looked at the picture. The moon was almost full and the face on the outside of it was clearly sketched. My face, he thought. He dropped down onto the grass, trying to figure out the words.

Was this why she'd been holding out the book to him? So he could see from her drawing how dumb looking he was? Or was there a message there she wanted him to see? Billy stared hard at the page, trying with all his might to guess what it meant, but nothing made sense.

He quickly flipped through the pictures and words on the earlier pages. One of them—the picture of the baby in the box—had been torn out. He could see where only the scalloped edges were left. On another page, he read his name, *Billy*. What had she written about him? Was it something bad?

The roses from the front yard smelled like something a person could eat at a circus, and the candy scent made Billy feel sick. He took a deep breath and started heading home, one foot in front of the other. He went along the walk, through the hedge, and onto the street, as if he were sleepwalking. A car honked as it passed, and he jumped out of the way.

"Same to you!" he yelled, anger burning like a wildfire in his throat. He reached into his pocket, pulled out Mrs. Schmidt's pennies, and flung them in the gutter. What good was it to make wishes? They never amounted to anything!

When he got to his apartment, he looked down with surprise at the yellow notebook in his hand. He'd meant to throw it back onto Natasha's steps. He went into his bedroom and dropped it on the floor, and then he heard water draining from the bathtub and soon his mother was calling.

"Billy? Let's have some lunch and then I'm going to try the afternoon at work, after all. Wanna swim at the pool?"

He pushed the notebook under his bed and took out the Typhoon and held it in the palm of his hand. Twenty-one tricks. He knew twenty-one tricks, but what good would that do? In the event of earthquakes, tidal waves, and tornados, what good, in the end, were a few tricks?

• • •

That afternoon, he sat on the couch beside Mr. Schmidt, tapping his feet against the carpet and watching *Wheel of Fortune*. He couldn't make up his mind who his favorite contestant was, and Mr. Schmidt was no help because he kept dozing off, leaning against a large pig pillow. Billy didn't really care, anyway, who won. He didn't care about anything.

"You're quiet today," said Mrs. Schmidt, coming in with

a plate of Rice Krispie squares. Billy just shook his head at them.

"And no cake! Something maybe is wrong, like a pig got your tongue?"

Billy smiled at that, and Mrs. Schmidt went on.

"How's things over there with that Romanian friend of yours?"

Billy shook his head again.

"I dunno. I guess she can talk, after all," he said, finally. "She just doesn't want to."

"There must have been a big sadness," said Mrs. Schmidt. "A big sadness came and wrapped itself around her voice, like a blanket. Her voice is still there, but it's just muffled up."

"Well you'd think things would be good for her," Billy burst out. "She lives over there in that house, and they have a big, gray car with lots of buttons on the dash. And there's this huge piano in their house, it's almost as big as the car! It's shiny, too! Natasha might have been sad before, when she was in that orphanage and missed her mom, but you'd think she'd be happy now."

"Something must have happened to make her remember the sadness," Mrs. Schmidt went on. "Something that made her open the door where the sadness lay, waiting. But that's how it is, with some things. You have to open the door and let them out."

Billy thought about that, about opening the door. He remembered what his mom had said about drinking when she was pregnant with him, and about his heart. She'd said he didn't have to worry about his heart, that it was better than most people's. And she'd said, "You can be who you want to be." That meant if he wanted to be an amazing yo-yo master, he should give it a try. But how could he be in the contest if he didn't have a sponsor? He thought about these things until the TV show was done, and then he went back home where he thought some more. He was quiet during supper, and his mom looked at him with a worried expression on her face, but she didn't say anything. Then he went to his room where he worked on the tricks. All twenty-one of them. And he could do them all, perfectly.

At bedtime he listened, suddenly longing for the sound of rain, but no rain fell. He tossed and turned, and finally slept, waking up in the thick gray night to the sound of the fridge humming. Every now and then a few doors opened and closed somewhere in the building, and he could hear the purring of cars as they drove past. All of them heading somewhere, anywhere but here.

Chapter Thirteen

On Thursday, Billy woke with a heavy feeling in his stomach. Natasha's notebook still lay on the floor of his room and his foot touched it when he stood up. He quickly stepped away and went into the bathroom where he heard his mother in the kitchen, making breakfast.

"I'm feeling better today," she called. "Must have been the heat. I'm going to work. Do you want to come and have a swim?"

"No," said Billy, from the bathroom. He wanted to yell at her that it was the day of the contest and remind her that he didn't have a sponsor, but he kept quiet. She didn't care. All Mom ever wanted to do was go to work.

"Hey, did you enter a draw? At the store?" she asked.

"What?" said Billy.

"A draw. At the store," his mother repeated.

"Oh. Yeah, I guess I did," said Billy, remembering putting his phone number on the little slip.

"Well, they called a little while ago." His mother came into the hallway and stood smiling at him as he came out of the bathroom. "And you won!"

"I did?" asked Billy, his heart lifting. What had he won? Was it a piano? A car?

"You won a year's supply of diapers!" his mother announced, giving him a quick hug. "What a great surprise!"

"Diapers," said Billy, astounded. "What are we gonna do with dumb old diapers?" What Eddie had said to him at school came back: *Reading baby words. Does the baby Billy wear a diaper too?*

"For the baby, silly," said his mom. "In a couple of months, those diapers are gonna be such a big help!"

"Oh," said Billy. He tried to muster a smile, but he just couldn't match his mother's enthusiasm. Diapers! Not a car. Not a piano. Just like everything else he did, he'd messed up again.

"I left five dollars in change on the counter," she said. "Go buy a couple of boxes of popsicles, and you can have two today."

He didn't answer and when he heard the door of the apartment click shut, he felt something like thunder explode inside him. He pushed the money off the counter onto the floor. Then he kicked two of the chairs over, and was going to push over a third, when he stopped himself. Mrs. Schmidt would come over to see what the noise was, and he didn't want to talk to her. He didn't want to talk to anyone.

"He's going to come," Billy said out loud. "He's going to come home and help me find a sponsor." But deep down, he knew it wasn't true. Dad wasn't going to come home. He wasn't going to come to the contest and play for him, either, just the way he hadn't taken him to the circus or called him on the telephone or even written him a letter. Not that Billy could have read a letter, even if his father had written one, but it would have been something. It would have been something.

Stupid contest! Billy thought, and stupid to think that he might have won. He ran back to his bedroom and looked at his ceiling, where the fault line was. "Go ahead!" he yelled. "Fall down. Tear apart! See if I care! This whole place could fall down and I wouldn't care!"

The silence after these words had a sharp edge to it that made him ache inside. He flopped down on his bed and then stood up, pressing his face against the window. Natasha wasn't sitting on her steps, where he thought she'd be. She was lying on her back on the lawn, looking at the sky.

Maybe she's waiting for the sky to fall, thought Billy with disgust. What good is it just hanging around all the time? Couldn't she go do something else? Natasha looked over his way and he pushed up the window, dangling out the notebook, and then pulling it back in and tossing it onto the bed.

Now she was standing on the grass. She was staring right up into his window. She knew he had the notebook—she'd seen it.

As he looked out, she waved her arms at him.

"Come out!" her arms seemed to say, "come out now!"

He stepped out of sight. Why should he go down to her? She couldn't help him. But maybe she just wanted her notebook back. Billy picked it up from the bed and went back to the window. She was still in her yard, waving her arms at him.

He leaned out the window and threw the notebook. It fell like a big moth, its pages flapping, and she ran towards it. That was all he saw before he yanked his curtains shut—the book diving like a big yellow moth, and Natasha, her arms outstretched, running towards it.

Chapter Fourteen

When he heard the screech of brakes and someone yelling, he opened his curtains. He couldn't believe what he saw. It was like something in the movies.

A car was stopped in the middle of the street, and a figure lay beside it. A small figure in a white lace dress. A woman got out of the car and crouched beside the figure.

"Call 911!" she yelled. "Somebody, call 911!"

Billy couldn't move. He imagined himself running for the phone, picking up the receiver, dialing. But he didn't. He just stood there, watching. Soon the door of Natasha's house opened, and Mrs. Arnold came running out. She was screaming.

After a few minutes, an ambulance came and the attendants moved Natasha onto a stretcher and took her away with Mrs. Arnold. A policeman got out of a police car and talked to the driver. Then he drove away, and the car slowly pulled out behind him.

Long after they had all vanished, Billy stood there, his knuckles white on the windowsill. He could still see the figure lying in the road. Even when he closed his eyes, he could see Natasha, lying there.

Why did it have to happen? Why did that car have to be there, just when she was running out? And why hadn't she looked? She'd run from behind the hedge without even looking! Stupid! It was such a stupid thing to do!

He stumbled around the apartment feeling the anger sloshing around inside his belly like water in a leaky boot.

Then he remembered the notebook. He looked out the window and saw it lying on the brittle grass. He went downstairs and picked it up. The pages were crumpled and hot. As he stared at them, he thought he smelled roses, but it was a sickly smell and his stomach twisted at the scent.

When the knock came at the door, he was sure it was Natasha's father, come to yell at him for taking her notebook.

"Go away," he said. "I'm busy."

"Billy?" said a voice. "Billy? Is your mother home?"

Billy opened the door and Mrs. Schmidt was standing there, with pink pig slippers on her feet.

"Is your mother home?" she repeated.

"No, she's at work," he said, not taking his eyes from her slippers.

"Oh," said Mrs. Schmidt. "Okay."

Billy took a quick look at her face. She didn't look okay. Her cheeks had white blotches on them, like someone had pressed pennies against her skin and then taken them away.

Billy didn't know what to say. He looked back at her feet, and finally she broke the silence.

"Maybe I will come in? For a minute?" she said. She reached up a hand to hold the door frame as she shuffled through and her arm was trembling so hard it took her a minute to cross into the apartment. "I just need to talk to someone for a little while. I got bad news."

Billy backed into the room. Bad news. That could only mean that Natasha was dead and Mrs. Schmidt had come to tell them. He tried to speak, but all that came out of his throat was a puff of air.

Mrs. Schmidt went into the kitchen. He followed, bending down and picking up the money he'd thrown on the floor. He put it in his pocket and then went over to the kitchen sink. He didn't want to hear what Mrs. Schmidt had come to say.

"It's Pork Chop," she said, and Billy turned as she carefully lowered herself into a chair. "They took him to the hospital in the night. I can go when my daughter, Daisy, comes, but she won't be here for another hour. It's hard, waiting."

"It's . . . it's . . . what?" said Billy.

"Pork Chop's in the hospital. I just . . . it's hard to wait by myself," said Mrs. Schmidt.

"It's not about Natasha?" said Billy.

"Natasha?" asked Mrs. Schmidt.

"She got . . . she got hit by a car, I think," said Billy.

"Hit by a car? That little neighbor girl? Oh, that's terrible!" said Mrs. Schmidt. "And you saw it happen?"

I caused it, thought Billy, but he didn't say that.

"It was right outside," he said.

"They must have taken her to the hospital, too," said Mrs. Schmidt. "Wait, I'll phone and find out how she is. Do you have a phone book?"

Billy got her the phone book and stood at the counter while she phoned. He could still see Natasha's body lying in the street. Held there like a penny in the dirt.

"Do you know her last name?" Mrs. Schmidt called out as she dialed the hospital.

"It's Arnold," said Billy, his dry tongue sticking to the roof of his mouth. "Natasha Arnold."

"Good thing this town has only one hospital," Mrs. Schmidt said. "Makes finding a patient so easy."

Billy heard her ask if Natasha Arnold was there and accepting visitors. He waited while she finished the conversation and hung up the phone.

"She can have visitors!" Mrs. Schmidt announced. "When my daughter arrives, you can come with us, if you like. Visiting hours start at one."

"She . . . she's not dead!" breathed Billy.

"I didn't ask what was what, but she's not in intensive care like my Pork Chop. That's a good sign," said Mrs. Schmidt.

"Okay," said Billy, not sure he wanted to go to the hospital but dizzy with relief that Mrs. Schmidt hadn't brought bad news about Natasha. Natasha was at the hospital and she was not dead. "Did Pork Chop have a hole in his heart?" he asked, rubbing through his T-shirt at the scar on his own chest. "Doctors can fix it, you know."

"It's his cancer," said Mrs. Schmidt. "It's real bad."

"But he's going to get better," said Billy. "He'll get better, soon."

"No, I don't think so," said Mrs. Schmidt in a voice as thin as a blade of old grass. "No, I don't think this time."

Billy didn't know what to say. He got up and got her a glass of water, taking as long as he could at the sink, but when he came back to the table she was standing.

"I'm okay, now," she said. "I've got my second wind. I'll be okay. Soon my daughter will come, and we'll go to the hospital. We have to look on the bright side, we have to hope. Hope springs eternal."

She lifted the glass to her lips, and Billy saw that she wasn't shaking any more. *Hope springs eternal.* The words had a kind of music in them that made Billy want to repeat them. They slid into his chest and curled up in the empty space that had been there ever since his father had left. Hope was something that, even when you were sad or mad, kept coming back. Like when you made a wish and it didn't come true but you wished for it anyway, and most of the time just making the wish made you feel better.

"Hope springs eternal," he repeated, and Mrs. Schmidt smiled.

Chapter Fifteen

The hospital was at the end of a parking lot and there was a big flower bed full of roses by the front door. They reminded Billy of disappointment, and he tried not to breathe as he walked past them and up the stairs, following Mrs. Schmidt and Daisy. He was carrying the yellow notebook, planning to give it back to Natasha as soon as he saw her. The lady at the desk told them which rooms they wanted, and Mrs. Schmidt took Billy to Natasha's room first.

"We'll ask if it's all right if you visit," she told him. "Her parents will probably be there."

Mr. and Mrs. Arnold were there, sitting in chairs one on either side of the bed. In the bed was a small shape covered by a white blanket. Her face was pale. Her eyes were closed.

"Is she dead?" Billy whispered brokenly, clutching the notebook in his hands.

"No, of course not," said Mrs. Arnold. "Just resting. She was very lucky."

"Is it okay if Billy comes in?" asked Mrs. Schmidt. "He wanted to make sure she was okay. My daughter will come back and get him in a little while."

"Well, just for a few minutes," said Mrs. Arnold, fanning herself with her purse. "I'm sure Natasha would like to see Billy when she decides to wake up."

Mrs. Schmidt gave him a little push towards the bed and then went back out into the hallway to look for Pork Chop's room.

"Is she really okay?" Billy asked, wiping a hand across his dry lips. The pancakes Mrs. Schmidt had fed him for lunch threatened to come up, and he swallowed, hard.

"She doesn't seem to want to be awake," said Mrs. Arnold, looking at her husband. "The doctor said . . . he said it was common in kids like her who have been through trauma. But she's here with us, and you'd think everything would be all right."

"It's my fault!" blurted Billy. "I made her run. I threw her notebook and she ran to get it. I guess . . . I guess a car was coming."

"It's that damn hedge," said Mr. Arnold. "I was planning to trim it one of these days. Cars just can't see past it!"

"But she should have looked before she crossed the street," said Mrs. Arnold. "It wasn't all—"

"I said it was my fault!" Billy cried, wanting to make them see. "I threw this notebook out my window and it belongs to her! I took it by accident, and then I kept it because I thought there was something in it about me. If I hadn't thrown it, she wouldn't have run into the street!"

There was a silence as Mr. and Mrs. Arnold looked at him.

"That was a hard thing for you to tell us, son," said Mr. Arnold, finally. "We do appreciate it."

"Well, it's just a broken arm," said Mrs. Arnold in a voice as lumpy as oatmeal. "Thank God. It could have been a lot worse." She looked at Natasha, then back at Billy, and then towards the window where pigeons were fluttering on the ledge.

The room was hot and Billy felt thirsty. He licked his lips and decided that if he were in the desert he'd wish for water. Water would be his first choice after all. He looked at the pitcher by the bed, but nobody offered him any. Finally he held out the notebook.

"She should have this back," he said.

Mr. Arnold reached out and took it.

"She's always writing in these things," he said. "Thanks, son, I'm sure she'll be glad to see it. Right, Natasha? You'll be glad to get this back?"

When Natasha neither stirred nor opened her eyes, Billy cleared his throat.

"It's a kind of journal," he said, shuffling from foot to foot. "It's got drawings in it, too. And I saw my name in it."

Mr. Arnold opened the notebook and looked at it.

"I see," he said. "She's called it a Moon Journal. She sure does spend a lot of time looking at the moon ever since they did that assignment in school last year. Remember, Mother? When they had to draw the moon every night?"

"Do you want to read it?" asked Billy. "She's got lots of stuff in there, about the moon."

"Well, I don't know if we should," said Mr. Arnold. "Maybe another time."

"It might put a little life into her," whispered Mrs. Arnold, staring at Natasha's closed eyes. "Do you want us to read your journal, dear?" she asked loudly.

Billy thought he detected a flicker in the closed lids, but he couldn't be sure.

"I'd like to know what it says," said Billy. "I'd read it myself, but my eyes are . . . are really tired right now. I saw my name in it," he said, again. He cleared his throat once more and kicked his foot against the bottom of the bed. "She's written something about me in there..." he said, his voice trailing off.

Mr. Arnold looked at him for a moment without saying anything, then looked at Natasha, and then at his wife. Finally, he gazed down at the journal.

"'Moon Journal, by Natasha Jelnick Arnold, Thursday July 6,'" he read, in a husky voice. "'Waning Crescent. There's only a sliver of the moon tonight, like a piece of cantaloupe. Soon the moon will disappear.'"

"That's a very smart description," broke in Mrs. Arnold. "A moon like a piece of cantaloupe. So poetic."

"What does it say next?" asked Billy.

Mr. Arnold glanced over at Natasha, from whom there had been no sound, and then resumed his reading.

"'Friday July 7. The very thinnest of crescent moons is out tonight. I wonder if it's sad to be disappearing.

"'Saturday July 8. New Moon tonight. The sky is black. It feels like I'll never see the moon again. The night is so empty. I feel empty, too.'"

"Okay, what about the next page," said Billy, shuffling from foot to foot beside the bed and craning his neck so he could see better.

There was a picture at the top of the next page, a thin fingernail of a moon, colored pale yellow.

"It says, 'Sunday July 9. The moon is showing tonight. It is a very thin Waxing Crescent. I saw it after dinner when I sat on the front steps. The boy across the street and his dad came home from the pool. They were wearing their trunks, and their hair was wet.'"

"That's me!" said Billy. "And my dad! We did go to the pool that night! That was before . . . before my dad left. We went home and had fried mushrooms."

"'Monday, July 10,'" Mr. Arnold went on. "'The moon is getting a bit larger. It was cool tonight. When it started to rain, they said I had to come in.'"

Billy nodded. "I remember when it rained that time."

"'Tuesday July 11. Too many clouds tonight. I didn't see the moon. Wednesday July 12. Cloudy again. No moon tonight. I am so disappointed. Thursday July 13. I saw the moon! It is a First Quarter. It looks like a section of a Christmas orange with some of the white peeling still on it.'"

"I remember when it looked like that," said Billy. "That wasn't so long ago."

"'Friday July 14,'" read Mr. Arnold. "'We are having a heat wave. It is a clear night and still warm. I saw the Big Dipper. The moon looked pure white tonight. Why is it white? You can see the craters on it. I wonder how the moon was made.'"

Mr. Arnold put the journal on his lap.

"How about that," he said to Mrs. Arnold. "She asks the darnedest questions, doesn't she?"

"You'd never guess she only learned English three years ago," said his wife. "She was such a quick learner. And so determined."

"She's pretty determined about this journal," said Mr. Arnold. "Imagine redoing a class assignment in the summer. It must have made an impression on her when she did it the first time."

"The moon is pretty important to her," said Billy. Mr. and Mrs. Arnold were watching their daughter and didn't take much notice of him.

"I heard a story once about how the moon was made," said Billy.

The Arnolds said nothing, and finally Billy went on.

"The moon was a shiny ball owned by an old lady. She kept it in a box. Raven stole the moon from them. Then he flew out the window with the moon in his beak." Billy stopped.

"Wait," he said. "Raven was a girl. I should have said: *She* flew out the window, with the moon in *her* beak."

Natasha shifted and a flicker of a smile lifted her cheek.

"Go on," said Mrs. Arnold, looking at her daughter hopefully, and then at Billy. "Go on, Billy. That's a very good story. I think Natasha would like you to finish it."

Billy tried to remember how his teacher had told the rest of the story. The next part had something to do with Saskatoon berries. Natasha's legs moved and she rolled over in bed, but her eyes were still shut.

"Please go on," said Mr. Arnold, not taking his eyes from his daughter.

"I remember it, now," Billy said. "But moons are not Saskatoon berries. They are not stones in a gravel pit. Moons are very big and very heavy. Raven got tired and threw the moon into the sky so she could rest. She said she would go get it when she wasn't tired anymore. But she forgot. And that's how the moon got into the sky."

"That's very nice, Billy," said Mr. Arnold, looking briefly his way. "Where did you hear that story?"

"My teacher, like I said before. He read us lots of those stories last year. Like how the camel got its hump, how the tiger got its stripes."

"Well, it's a good story," said Mr. Arnold, his eyes back on Natasha. "You have a good memory."

"Read the rest of the journal," Billy said. "Please."

When there was no response from Natasha, her father went on.

"Well, there's more about Friday, July 14," he said. "'I saw the moon first this morning, and the boy across the street came over and looked at it, too. He lives in the red-brick apartment building. He is funny. He can do lots of tricks with his yo-yo.'"

"That's about me! That's me!" exclaimed Billy.

Mrs. Arnold looked at him.

"You had your yo-yo at our place one day, didn't you?" she asked.

Billy nodded, and reached into his pocket to make sure the Typhoon was still there. It was. He looked over at Mr. Arnold who was beginning to read again.

"'Saturday July 15,'" he read. "'Day by day, the moon is getting bigger. Tonight it was still hot when I went to bed. I wonder if the moon feels too heavy when it's full.

"'Sunday July 16. It was hot again tonight. I couldn't sit on the step until after supper because the cement burned my legs. I saw the boy go out once today, and then come home with a bag from the store. I bet he bought something for his mother. The moon is getting bigger each night. The boy's name is Billy and he told me a story about how the moon was too heavy to hang onto.'"

"I knew I was in it!" said Billy, moving over beside Mr. Arnold. "There's my name!" He pointed to his name on the page. "There, it says *Billy*!"

"'Monday July 17. It is still hot,'" continued Mr. Arnold. "'The moon is a Waxing Gibbous, and is almost a Full Moon. It is the color of a goldfish. I saw Billy's dad coming out of their apartment with some bags of stuff and a guitar. Sometimes he looks nice and sometimes he doesn't. Today he doesn't.'" Mr. Arnold's voice faltered. He put down the journal and took a handkerchief out to wipe his sweaty forehead.

"We'll read this another time, okay?" he said. "Natasha's probably tired of listening, now."

"No, please!" said Billy. "Just finish! It's only a few more pages."

Mr. Arnold quickly flipped through the rest of the book.

"It doesn't really make a lot of sense—" he began.

"Please finish it!" said Billy. Mr. Arnold studied him for a moment, and then went back to where they had left off.

"Okay. Well, we're almost done," he said, eyeing his daughter. "'Tuesday July 18. Billy and I went to see Dad. Billy wanted to ask him about being his sponsor for the contest. Then Dad drove us home. We went out for dinner, but I can never eat enough to please them.'" Mrs. Arnold made a funny noise in her throat, and when Billy looked at her, she was looking the other way.

"'When we came home I watched for the moon from my window. At first there were too many clouds, but I knew it was there, waiting for me. Like she waits for me. I miss her. I wonder if she is looking at the moon tonight and thinking of me.'"

Mr. Arnold stopped reading and cleared his throat.

"That's all?" said Billy.

"'In the desert,'" Mr. Arnold read, "'if I could only take one thing with me, I would take a friend. Because that's the most important thing a person can have.'"

Billy stared at the picture Natasha had drawn and realized suddenly that she was talking about him. He was her friend in the desert. In the picture he was wearing the same clothing he was wearing now—blue shorts and a red T-shirt.

"And then it says, 'Wednesday, July 19.' But this page doesn't make much sense. Underneath the date it just says, 'I will help you.'"

"Who will she help?" asked Mrs. Arnold.

"That's all she wrote," said Mr. Arnold. "Just, 'I will help you.'"

Mrs. Arnold got a Kleenex out of her purse and dabbed at her eyes.

"I think it's me!" said Billy. "She was trying to show me the notebook when she knew I couldn't find a sponsor for the contest. I think she wrote it to me. But—" he swallowed hard. "I can't read those words. I can't read, you know."

"There are so many puzzles," said Mrs. Arnold, softly. "And we can't seem to do enough. We can't seem to make things right."

"Hush, now," said Mr. Arnold. "We're doing the best we can."

"But she won't even talk to us anymore!" Mrs. Arnold went on. "She won't tell us what's wrong! She has those tears in her eyes all the time, but she never cries. She didn't even cry when she broke her arm. And she never really smiles, either."

"Hush, Mother," said Mr. Arnold. "She's just got a lot to get over. It'll get better. You'll see."

"But they're keeping her here for observation," said his wife. "Most children with a broken arm would be in and out. But they're keeping her and all she does is just lie there . . ."

Mr. and Mrs. Arnold seemed to have forgotten Billy was there. He wanted to run. He wanted to run out of that room as fast as he could, but his body wouldn't do what he wanted it to. It was as if his feet were rooted to the floor.

It struck him that maybe they were in a place like the

desert right now, and if he was Natasha's friend, he should help her if he could.

"Maybe she's got a secret," he blurted. "A secret that she thinks she shouldn't tell."

Mr. and Mrs. Arnold turned towards him. He had their attention. Even Natasha, with her eyes shut, seemed to be listening.

"And some secrets are pretty heavy," Billy went on. "They're as heavy as the moon. Like when I took that money from my mom and then she thought Dad stole it. Those are the secrets that you gotta give up. Natasha taught me that. She said I should tell my mom, and I did."

Mrs. Arnold looked at him, still dabbing at her eyes.

"Natasha talks to you?" she asked, brokenly.

"Well, kind of. She can tell me things even if she doesn't speak. You just gotta know how to listen that way."

"Do you know something?" she asked in a shaky voice. "Something we should know?"

Billy started to shake his head, but then he looked at Natasha, who had opened her eyes.

"Why don't you say?" he said to her.

She shook her head.

"Do you want me to say it for you?" Billy asked. "It'll make you feel better."

Natasha looked at him, her eyes huge in her small, pale face. Then she nodded.

"It's about her mother," said Billy. "Her real mother," he said, looking at Mrs. Arnold. "She isn't dead. She used to come visit. It was a secret."

He picked up the Moon Journal that was lying on the bed and looked inside.

"There used to be a picture in here of when her mother left her at the orphanage. And her mother came back and visited her. Natasha told me. And her mother's name was Natasha, too!" The back cover of the notebook fell open, and Billy saw that there was another picture there. It was of a woman and a girl standing together, holding hands, under a full moon.

"I bet she came to visit every time there was a full moon! Right, Natasha?"

Mrs. Arnold gave a little gasp, and her purse tumbled off her lap and onto the floor.

"How do you know?" asked Mr. Arnold, his voice loud in the little room. "How do you know this?" Billy held out the picture. Mr. Arnold looked at it and then at Natasha. Natasha gripped her blanket in her hands, and then nodded her head.

"Your mother's alive?" asked Mr. Arnold. "But we thought . . . the orphanage said—"

A tear slid down Natasha's cheek and dropped onto the blanket.

"Was she . . . was she there when we came and got you?" Mrs. Arnold asked in a thick voice. "Did she know that you were going away?"

Natasha looked at the window and shook her head. More tears fell, and she leaned over and sobbed into the blanket.

"She couldn't look after her," said Billy, "because she

was too poor. But she'd come and visit. Whenever there was a full moon. Right?"

Mrs. Arnold got up very slowly and went over and sat on the bed beside Natasha. Gently, she gathered Natasha onto her lap.

"It was the journal," she said softly to her husband. "The doctor's been asking about anything that might have gotten her worked up last fall, and I think it was doing the moon journal."

"It opened the door," said Billy, but nobody paid him any attention. After a few minutes, Billy said, "I really like it when my mom rubs my back. But you have to go hard around the shoulder blades. And then tickle, but just a little bit."

A sound came from Natasha that wasn't crying. She sat up and Billy saw that she was laughing. It was the sound of meadowlarks, and he smiled. Everything was going to be okay.

"And I thought of something!" said Billy. "That Kids' Hope Foundation. They give kids who are sick a chance to make a wish and get it. Natasha could go back. She could go back and see her mother, if she likes." He thought of his father, of the day when he'd had a chance to say good-bye, but hadn't. "Maybe she could say good-bye," he finished, solemnly.

Natasha looked at him, her expression making Billy wish he'd thought of this the moment he'd met her, the instant he'd seen those big glistening eyes, even though he hadn't known, then, what was the matter. He tried to find the right words to go on.

"You are who you are," he said, finally. "You can do anything you want. As long as you put your mind to it." He struggled for a minute, searching for something else. Then he said, in a voice that sounded like his own and yet somehow wasn't his own, a deeper, more confident voice than his old one: "Hope springs eternal." And Natasha smiled a real smile.

Chapter Sixteen

When Mrs. Schmidt's daughter dropped Billy off at the apartment, he tried to remember his manners.

"I hope your father's going to be better, soon," he said. "It's good that Mrs. Schmidt was feeding him that soup she brought. He'll like that. Even though there's vegetables in it. She makes good soup. She makes good everything."

Daisy smiled.

"Thanks, Billy. The doctor says if we can get his strength up, he might be able to come home in a few days. The new medication might help a bit. He's not going to get better, but he might get well enough to come home for a while."

"Good luck," said Billy, closing the car door behind him. He trudged up the walk, thinking about things. As he opened the door of their building he suddenly couldn't stand the thought of going alone into the empty apartment. He stepped back into the yard, the bright sunlight making him squint. For a moment it looked like Dad was coming up the walk. He blinked. It was only the mailman. Billy turned away.

The street was as still and hot as a desert, the leaves hanging from the trees like broken promises. Billy walked along in the gutter, kicking at the elm seeds and dirt that lay against the curb. There were no earthworms there today. Mrs. Schmidt would say it was so hot you could fry sausages on the sidewalk, but he wasn't so sure. An egg, maybe, but not sausages.

A humming noise filled the air and Billy could see two workmen trimming the caragana hedge along Natasha's front yard. They were cutting the bushes so low that Billy figured he could easily step right over them.

He thought about what Natasha had written. It was nice to think about being her friend. She hadn't written anything bad about him after all. Not like the kids at school. Suddenly he wondered if those notes really had said bad things. Maybe they hadn't.

And anyhow, people could change. One day they could seem like they didn't want to be your friend, and another day they could change their minds. Like Eddie, and the way he'd helped Billy pay the registration fee. Something about that made Billy feel uneasy, though. Now he wondered if Eddie hadn't been tricking him somehow. Mom had said there was nothing at all in the pamphlet about a registration fee.

Billy walked along until he saw red and white petunias at his feet and realized, quite suddenly, that he was at the park. He started to turn back towards home, but music caught his attention. He looked over towards the bandstand, and saw a crowd of people. In a flash, Billy remembered the contest. He'd missed his chance, and now it was too late. As if pulled by an invisible string, he walked over to the crowd.

"Hey, Billy, you're just in time," called a voice. He looked up. It was Eddie Mundy.

"I'm collecting from all the participants. Five bucks, cash." He smiled at Billy.

Billy started to say that he didn't have five bucks when he remembered the popsicle money. He felt one pocket. All he had there was the Typhoon. He felt the other pocket and his fingers recognized coins. He reached in his hand and drew them out.

"Just like taking candy from a baby," muttered Eddie.

"I'm not a baby!" Billy cried. Suddenly he felt that giving Eddie the money was the wrong thing to do.

"Are you sure?" he demanded. "Are you sure you're collecting for the contest? Did everybody pay?"

Eddie's smile grew wider. "Sure, kid. You bet."

"You're not telling the truth!" Billy said, stuffing the money back into his pocket.

"Who you callin' a liar!" yelled Eddie. "You little runt!"

Before he knew it, Eddie had grabbed him around the neck. Instinctively, Billy's arms went up, tightening his neck muscles and giving himself a chance to maneuver. He turned quickly sideways, breaking free of Eddie's grasp and sending the bigger boy off balance. As Eddie toppled away from him, Billy slammed him on the back with all his might. Eddie fell, his nose hitting the pavement so hard that blood sprayed out.

"And don't try to take my money again!" Billy yelled, turning and running for the bandstand.

"And the next act we have is Billy Ray the Amazing Yo-yo Master," bellowed a voice into a microphone. Billy stopped running. He couldn't take part in the contest. He had no sponsor. He saw Samantha smiling at him and felt hands push him forward until he was on the stage in front of the microphone. As if in a trance, he took the yo-yo out of his pocket.

"Let's hear it for BILLY RAY, THE AMAZING YO-YO MASTER!" said the announcer, and everyone clapped. Billy looked out into the audience. He licked his dry lips and remembered how Natasha had liked seeing his tricks. She'd even written about them in her journal. Slowly and carefully he wrapped the string. Then he held the Typhoon in his hand, as if he were going to begin, but his arms and legs felt hollow. All his power was gone.

"Come on, you can do it!" yelled a voice from the crowd, and Billy licked his lips again. He thought hard, but he couldn't remember any of the tricks. Out of the twenty-one he'd learned, not one came back to him now.

"He's teaching the yo-yo to sleep," said someone else. "He's learned that trick good!" A few people laughed.

Billy looked around desperately. He didn't know what to do. He took one shaky step towards the edge of the stage and then stopped. He couldn't just give up. What about all the practicing he'd done?

Billy's legs were trembling so much that he could hardly control them. He wished feverishly for a real earthquake so he could be swallowed up and disappear off the face of the earth.

"Let's get this show on the road!" came another catcall. "We're gettin' old!"

Suddenly people started cheering Billy on, and there was a ripple of clapping, but it didn't help.

Then there was a sound he recognized, a voice, calm and sure. Someone was singing. It was a song he knew.

> *Well it's a one for the money,*
> *Two for the show,*
> *Three to get ready, now,*
> *Go cat go . . .*

Billy stepped back in front of the microphone and let the rhythm of the song move the power back into his body. Then he tried one of the tricks. It worked. He tried another. It worked fine.

> *You can do anything,*
> *But stay off my blue suede shoes.*

The song went on, lifting him, carrying him forward through the tricks, one after the other.

Once, Billy faltered and he couldn't remember what trick came next, but the song kept going, and in a few moments he tried *Shoot the Moon*. Perfect. He tried *Walk the Dog*. Perfect. Then he tried *Rock the Cradle*. Perfect. He let the words lead him until he'd done all the tricks, all twenty-one of them. *Water Slider. Moon Shadow. Pancake Flip*. Even *CN Tower*. And all of them were exactly right.

But doncha
Step on my blue suede shoes.
You can do anything,
But stay off my blue suede shoes.

When he was finished, the audience clapped wildly and a few people whistled. He looked behind him. Dad had to be there, singing. But the stage was empty. He looked out at the audience, searching the faces one after another, but he couldn't see his father anywhere.

Chapter Seventeen

Billy went and stood at the edge of the crowd, still looking for his dad. The harder he looked, the more he had a funny feeling that his dad wasn't there. He pushed this thought out of his mind but the harder he pushed, the quicker it kept coming back.

There were two more acts, and then the show was done. He'd missed most of it, but at least he'd arrived in time for his performance. He felt pins and needles run up and down his arms and legs at the sheer excitement of having done his act in front of all these people.

The judges spent a few minutes talking and then one of them walked up to the announcer and gave him an envelope.

"All right, ladies and gentleman. I would like to announce the winner of today's talent contest. But first, let me tell you that seven hundred and fifty dollars has been raised for this year's charity, the Kids' Hope Foundation! Good work, everyone!

"Now, regarding the contest winner, congratulations to . . . BILLY RAY, THE AMAZING YO-YO MASTER and, in addition to that, a very fine singer!"

Billy felt as if he had just swallowed an egg, shell and all. He had performed all by himself, the singing and everything! He couldn't believe it, and a warm rush of pride filled him, leaving no room for any of the natural disasters which always seemed to be hovering.

I am who I am, he thought. *I can do whatever I want, as long as I put my mind to it.*

As he joyfully climbed the steps to the stage, someone called out to the announcer, "Wait, there's a problem."

The announcer talked with one of the judges while Billy stood, bewildered, on the stage, his hands in his pockets.

"Sorry for the delay, folks," said the announcer, coming back to stage centre. "But we have to make a change in our choice of winner. Apparently Billy Ray hasn't handed in his sponsor sheet, which disqualifies him from the contest."

He looked at Billy, a sad expression on his face.

"I'm sorry, Billy Ray. Rules are rules. Please step down. Instead, I invite Maya Rockthunder up to claim the prize for her Irish dancing."

Billy stumbled off the stage, and then watched as Maya claimed her prize, an envelope which, he knew, contained the twenty-five dollars.

He expected to feel badly. He waited for the rush of disappointment he was sure would come. But it didn't. Instead he felt lighter than air. They thought he'd been good enough to win. Even though he didn't have a sponsor, even though Dad hadn't been there, he had done all twenty-one tricks, and he'd won. It wasn't the money that was important. The important thing was this feeling, this feeling that for once he was good enough. He touched his hand to his head in a kind of salute to the winner, and then turned. Right into the plump chest of Mr. Arnold.

"Son, I'm really sorry," he panted. "I have the form you gave me right here. I did fill it in, but is it too late? I could talk to someone . . ."

Billy looked over at Maya Rockthunder, whose family was standing around congratulating her.

"No," he said. "It's okay. Leave it."

Mr. Arnold studied him for a moment, his red cheeks bobbing.

"You have a good heart, Billy," he said, finally.

"Tell Natasha I'll be keeping track of the moon for her. Until she comes home. Tell her to get better soon."

"I will, son," said Mr. Arnold gruffly. "And Billy?"

Billy looked at Mr. Arnold for a moment as the big man struggled for words.

"Thanks," Mr. Arnold said, finally. "Thanks . . . for all you've done for my little girl."

Billy watched him head back towards the gray car. He started to walk down the path, but saw Eddie, standing at the end of it.

I think I'll just go the other way, thought Billy, and then he was startled to see Eddie turn and walk away first. Eddie, walking away from him, was a sight that Billy had never thought he'd see, not in a million years. He smiled, then laughed, and then rolled on the grass with pure joy.

When he looked up, he saw, in the middle of the blue sky, the white ghost of a full moon. Hanging there, like a memory.

"It'll be okay," he said, his voice echoing in his ears as if it rang to the other side of the world and back. "It'll be okay. Just you wait!"

As if in answer, a meadowlark that was sitting on the branch of a nearby elm burst into song. Billy turned his body around on the grass until he could see the bird. It wasn't anything special, just an old brown bird with a pale yellow belly and a black V on its throat. And yet it made this amazing sound. He watched it for a while until it flew away, and then he rolled over and got up. It was time to be heading home. Maybe he could teach Mom how to make those fried mushrooms. They'd sure taste good right about now.

Seal of armour
Glyph of MR
Mark of armor

Percentage health Quit

Praise for Beverly Brenna's *Wild Orchid.*

"This is an honest, insightful, and compelling read." 4/4
– CM REVIEW

". . . this book is geared towards ability rather than
disability and is a highly recommended read."
– CANCHILD INTRANET

"This is a wonderful novel about being different."
– WHITE PINE AWARDS READING CLUB

Wild Orchid has been shortlisted for the:
Saskatchewan Book Awards
White Pine Awards
Canadian Library Assoc. Young Adult Book Award
Willow Awards (Sycra Awards)

Beverley Brenna is a Saskatchewan special education teacher who lives on an acreage near Saskatoon with her husband and three sons. Her previous titles for children include *Daddy Longlegs at Birch Lane*, *Spider Summer*, and *The Keeper of the Trees*. Her YA title *Wild Orchid* was shortlisted for a Young Adult Book Award from the Canadian Library Association as well as for a White Pine Award and the Manitoba Readers' Choice Award; it is also a starred selection from the Canadian Children's Book Centre. In addition to writing for young people, Brenna publishes prose and poetry for adults.

For more information, consult the author's website at www.beverleybrenna.com.